THE SECRET OF THE TEN BALES

by Anthony Parsons

Published by DEAN & SON, LTD
© Fleetway Publications Ltd 1968

Made and Printed in Great Britain by Purnell & Sons, Ltd.
Paulton (Somerset) and London

603 03503 5

CONTENTS

CONTENTS

CHAPTER 1

WHY THE MURDER OF A YOUNG CLERK?

THE whole thing began with the murder of a shipping clerk in a cul-de-sac off Fenchurch Street.

When the police arrived, the body was lying sprawled out with its feet and legs in the road, and its head and shoulders resting on the broken pavement. It was face downwards, and sopping wet, and in the opinion of the doctor had been lying there for at least five hours.

"And another thing," he told Superintendent Jarvis when the latter arrived from the Yard. "This lad was not strangled, but garrotted."

"Garrotted?" echoed the superintendent.

"Yes. Look at this! See that long, narrow bruise across the gullet? Now look at the back of his neck—not a mark—eh? Not even a slight discoloration?"

"Well?"

"That means that pressure was applied only to the throat, whereas in ordinary manual strangulation the killer's fingers exert pressure on the back of the neck exactly as his thumbs exert pressure on the gullet. See what I mean?"

"And in this case they haven't?"

"No. It looks to me as though somebody crept up behind the lad, slipped a walking stick or something similar across his throat and pulled back hard—in other words, garrotted him. And that's unusual in this country."

Jarvis nodded, and looked about him. Haires Court was no beauty spot at the best of times, but at night, in the rain and mist, it struck a really sinister note. Great, black warehouses loomed up drear and gaunt upon three

5

sides of it, and upon the fourth was Water Lane—one of those small turnings leading through from Fenchurch Street into Leadenhall Street.

"Anything in his pockets, Wilson?" he asked his assistant inspector.

"Not a thing, sir. Absolutely cleaned out and washed up. And a mere kid, at that!"

"Judging by his hands and clothes I'd say he was a clerk," the surgeon volunteered. "And since he isn't a day above nineteen, it's ten to one that he lived at home. In that case, somebody will soon be making inquiries for him."

It was then close on midnight, and at two in the morning a call was put through to Superintendent Jarvis at the Yard to the effect that a man named Newman was at Brixton police station making inquiries for his son, Gerald Newman, aged nineteen, who had not returned from his work in the City. It was feared that he had met with an accident. Jarvis went out and interviewed the man, and an hour later was in possession of all the facts.

Gerald Newman was nineteen and a few months—a clean-living lad, a sportsman, a leading light of the local Rugger club. He was employed by Messrs. Tanner & Wild, shippers, of Fenchurch Street, where he had been working for the last three years. As far as his father knew he had not an enemy in the world, was not interested in girls, and neither smoked nor drank. There seemed to be no earthly reason why anyone should want to kill the lad.

"Yet someone has killed him," Wilson said. "And not only killed him, but cleared out his pockets. Question is: What was he carrying?"

"Probably money or something belonging to the firm he worked for," Jarvis opined. And the first thing next morning he went down personally to interview Messrs. Tanner & Wild. He saw Mr. Tanner—a short, elderly, rubicund little man, who promptly rang for a Mr. Bradley, head of the department in which the murdered youth had worked. Yes, Gerald Newman was a junior shipping clerk in his department. His work lay mainly with documents, bills of lading and the like, work which took him frequently into the docks.

"Was he in the docks yesterday?" Jarvis asked.

"Yes," Bradley said. "He was there in the afternoon. He went down to the *Indrabrama* to get receipts for various consignments aboard that vessel. He got back here at four o'clock."

"Did he mention anything untoward—trouble or anything?"

"Nothing at all, superintendent. He brought back the signatures he had gone for, dealt with everything in the usual manner, and went off home. As a matter of fact, I left the office with him."

"What time would that be?"

"As near as makes no matter, ten minutes past six. He was in a hurry, I remember. Had a meeting of his Rugger club or something out at Brixton."

"Was that the last you saw of him?"

"Yes; I went to the station, and he went off to post the mail in Leadenhall Street. That was part of his job, by the way, posting the mail. He caught the quarter to seven post every night at the box there. It is a rule of the firm."

Jarvis thought rapidly. At ten minutes past six, Newman had left the office to post the firm's mail in Leadenhall Street—but he had never got there. He had been scuppered on his way through Water Lane—strangled, and his body thrown into the cul-de-sac known as Haires Court. He must have been carrying the mail when he met his death.

Where was the mail now?

"Good gad!" Mr. Tanner exclaimed when he mentioned the matter. "I hadn't thought of that." He remembered signing two cheques which had gone off to post last night, but when he rang up the people concerned, he found that the cheques had duly arrived. "So it couldn't have been the cheques they were after!" he beamed with relief.

"And he must have posted the mail after all," gloomed Jarvis. "Posted it and turned back again—in spite of his hurry to get to that Rugger meeting. What else was in the mail?"

"Oh, just the ordinary stuff," Bradley answered. "Letters, invoices, receipts perhaps, documents——"

"What documents?"

"Well, insurance documents and the like. Bills of lading and so on. I can tell you what they were." He thought for a moment. "There were ten bales of cotton-piece goods to Ram Dass, of Bombay, and three cases of engineers' tools for Walter Hindman, of Karachi—both lots aboard the *Indrabrama*. As a matter of fact," he added, "those were the goods for which Newman went to get receipts from the docks, yesterday afternoon."

"Receipts from whom?"

"The skipper, of course—for the bills of lading."

"What exactly is a 'bill of lading?' Briefly, I mean." Bradley smiled.

"Well briefly," he said, "if you shipped a car to the Emperor of China, the bill of lading is the document he would require to show the skipper before he could collect the car at the other end."

"So that anyone presenting a bill of lading to the captain of a ship can collect whatever goods are on that bill of lading? Is that the idea?"

"In practice, yes. There are formalities, of course, but where the firms are known to the Customs people and the shipping people generally—yes, a bill of lading is all you need to collect the goods."

"That's what I mean. Now then, what about these bills of lading that young Newman was taking to post last night?"

Mr. Tanner smiled.

"I catch your drift, superintendent," he said. "And had the stuff been cases of bullion—yes, there might have been something in the idea; but they weren't. The ten bales of cotton-piece goods were for our best Indian customer, one of the biggest importers in the trade. The other was for Hindman & Co., the big garage proprietors over there. And in any event, if anyone wanted to steal a bale of cotton-piece goods or a few engineers' tools, he'd steal them from the docks or from the warehouse. He wouldn't let them go to India, and then have to go out there after them!"

Jarvis supposed not. That didn't make sense. Apart from which, if Newman had posted the cheque part of the mail, the inference was that he had posted the lot, and therefore he had been alive when he reached Leadenhall Street at some time prior to a quarter to seven.

Why, then, had he turned back? Why hadn't he hurried on to his Rugger meeting at Brixton?

That looked queer to Jarvis, and he checked up on the matter. He visited the two firms mentioned, and managed to retrieve the envelopes in which the cheques had arrived. Then, to his surprise, he found that whatever young Newman might have done upon every other night of his life, upon the night of his death he had missed the post!

The postmark on each of those envelopes was 7.30!

"Guess he wasn't the industrious apprentice after all!" Wilson grinned. "Guess he stopped to have a drink somewhere."

"He didn't drink, according to his father," Jarvis reminded him tartly.

"Nor did I, at his age—according to my father!" Wilson retorted. "But in any case, we don't know that he did post those letters. The other chap might have posted them. He might have killed Newman in Water Lane, taken the letters from his dead body, and later on posted them himself."

"Why?"

"Well, to mess things up for us, sir. To hide his trail a bit, and confuse his purpose."

That evening, the papers came out with screaming headlines. It was inconceivable that a mere youth could be robbed and murdered in the heart of the City at a time when hundreds of thousands of Londoners were streaming homewards. They appealed for anyone who had seen him to come forward and help the police; but no one came. Neither then nor in the days that followed did a single person come forward with the slightest information.

Jarvis and Wilson wore themselves to shreds. Not a stone was left unturned. Every single letter written by Tanner and Wild that day was checked to its destination and found correct—all save the foreign letters, and those, of course, were already on the high seas, and could not be got at. But beyond the fact that every one of those letters bore the 7.30 time stamp, nothing emerged from the check. It was impossible to prove whether Newman himself had posted them, or whether they had been posted by his murderer.

At the end of a week the position was one of complete stalemate.

At the end of a month, the Gerald Newman murder had passed by imperceptible degrees into the limbo of London's unexplained and undiscovered crimes. And there, likely enough, it would have remained, had not Tanner & Wild received an urgent cable from their Indian customer, Ram Dass, demanding to know what had become of the ten bales of cotton-piece goods ordered by him nearly eight weeks ago.

Mr. Tanner passed the cable to his indent department for comment. Bradley himself looked up the shipment, and felt a strange little shiver run down his spine when he realised that the shipment of those particular goods had been Gerald Newman's last job on earth. He had gone down to the *Indrabrama* upon the afternoon of the day of his death. Swiftly he turned up the files. No, he had made no mistake. There was the copy, and the original bill of lading had been despatched to Ram Dass the same day. That bill of lading had been among the letters

Newman had been taking to post when he met his death. The only other bill of lading had been one made out at the same time for engineers' tools, for Hindman & Co., of Karachi, and those had been duly delivered. Of all the letters Newman had taken to post that night, only this one bill of lading remained unaccounted for.

"Nonsense!" Mr. Tanner said when Bradley rather breathlessly made his report. "Don't be melodramatic, man! A thousand things might have happened to it. Who'd want to murder for ten bales of cheap cotton-piece goods, anyhow? Cable Ram Dass that the stuff was shipped on the *Indrabrama*, and that the bill of lading was sent out on the 11th of last month. See what he says."

"Very good, sir." Bradley dispatched the cable, and the next day received an answer. No bill of lading had arrived in India, but inquiries at the Customs showed that someone had taken delivery of the ten bales, using Ram Dass' name and Ram Dass' bill of lading. To whom had they sent that bill of lading?

Mr. Tanner fumed and swore. All this mystery was doing his business no good. He cabled that the bill of lading had been despatched to Ram Dass according to instructions and in the ordinary way of business, and that if anyone had collected the ten bales in Bombay, using that bill of lading, the theft had occurred in Ram Dass' office. Ram Dass cabled back denying all knowledge of the bill of lading and holding Tanner & Wild responsible for his loss.

Then something else happened. An officer of the Special Branch called round upon Mr. Tanner, acting upon instructions from the Government of India, to inquire for details of ten bales of cotton-piece goods shipped by Tanner & Wild in the *Indrabrama* to the order of Ram Dass, of Bombay. It appeared that the stuff had been taken by a trick from the Customs shed and sent up-country by rail to Peshawar. Unfortunately, the train had been deliberately derailed and attacked by train-robbers, who had opened the ten bales of cotton-piece goods, partially burnt them, shot down the white guard of the train, and then decamped. Ram Dass denied all knowledge of the consignment, and now the authorities wanted a detailed account of what was in those bales, when they were shipped, where they were baled, and information as to the bill of lading which apparently had gone astray.

"They seem a bit jumpy over something out there, sir," the officer smiled. "Looks like a spot of trouble blowing up."

Mr. Tanner mopped his brow and thought rapidly. No doubt about it, Newman's death and those ten bales of cotton-piece goods were mixed up together. Someone had killed Newman for the sake of the bill of lading covering those ten bales; but a fool could see that there was more to it than that! As he had said in the beginning, who would commit murder for the sake of a paltry ten bales of cotton-piece goods? Nobody! Therefore those ten bales could not have been what they seemed.

"But I'm not to blame for that!" he told the officer stoutly. "All we did was to ship the stuff that was sent to us from Manchester. The bales were consigned to our warehouse, marked for shipment, and duly put aboard the *Indrabrama*."

"How long were they lying in your warehouse?" the officer asked.

"You mean——" Little Mr. Tanner gasped. "You mean that—you're suggesting they—you're trying to hint that they were tampered with?" he got out at last.

"I'm trying to get at the truth," the other answered in his quiet manner. "There was evidently something radically wrong with the things. Question is—what?"

"I suggest that you approach the manufacturers, sir!"

"I'm going to—don't you worry! There's going to be an almighty bust-up about these ten bales of cotton-piece goods, before we're through. A murder on this side; a murder and a hold-up over there! Not too good, Mr. Tanner! Something very fishy about it all."

And when that same day Scotland Yard reopened the whole of that half-forgotten Newman affair, Mr. Tanner was fain to agree. He put through a personal call to the Manchester manufacturer, and discussed things with him in detail. Ram Dass, a valued customer, had been placed in a distinctly awkward position in India. The manufacturer and Mr. Tanner himself were under suspicion here. The publicity would do neither firm any good—couldn't they do something about it?

"Better engage a good solicitor to look after our joint interests," advised the Manchester man.

"Don't you believe it!" retorted Mr. Tanner. "There'll be no peace here until the affair is settled and the real criminal brought to justice. What we want is someone who will solve the whole wretched problem for us."

"Well, have you got anybody in mind?"

Mr. Tanner nodded. He had had a gentleman in mind for some few days past, if only he could be induced to take on the case.

"A man," he said over the wire, "who has undertaken one or two jobs for us in the past, and done remarkably well. The only question is, can we get him?"

"Who is he?" asked the man in the North.

"Sexton Blake," said Mr. Tanner. "The smartest man in England."

CHAPTER 2

SEXTON BLAKE'S DISCOVERY

BLAKE was at dinner when Mr. Tanner called round at the Baker Street address. The remains of one of Mrs. Bardell's famous pies stood derelict before him, and he was just sipping his solitary glass of wine when the bell rang and she trotted in to inform him that a Mr. Tanner wished to see him.

"But let him wait, sir," she said with a glance at the pie. "You finish your meal, sir."

Blake's lean face cracked to a smile.

"The only occasion upon which I feel inclined to regret my slimness," he said, "is when you make one of your pies. If only I were a Daniel Lambert now——" He smiled again as he got to his feet. "You kept him waiting?"

"Yes—if you're sure you've finished," she sighed regretfully.

"But I must leave something for Tinker, Mrs. Bardell! He isn't back yet?"

"Not yet—no."

"Well, tell him to wait for me when he does come back —if I'm still engaged, that is. And, I say——"

"Yes, Mr. Blake?"

"I have a feeling that I shall be needing my tropical kit shortly. If you've nothing better to do, you might give it a look over."

"But——"

"No, it's only a feeling!" he smiled. "Nevertheless, I have it—and my feelings are seldom wrong."

He reached for his pipe, stuffed it into the pocket of his dressing-gown, and went off to the consulting-room.

Mr. Tanner rose at his entry and held out his hand.

"Sorry to call on you at this hour of the night, Mr.

Blake," he apologised, "but I couldn't go home until I'd seen you."

"About that Newman business?" Blake asked, motioning the other to a chair.

Mr. Tanner paused, blinked for a moment, then shrugged his shoulders and sat down. He had had dealings with Sexton Blake before.

"Right first time," he conceded. "The fact is, Mr. Blake, the whole thing has become too hot for us. Detectives are smelling round the place all day, the Special Branch has started making diligent inquiries about us all over the city, and what with one thing and another it's time something was settled. You know how young Newman was killed?"

"I know that he was found dead in Haires Court, and that he worked in your offices," Blake admitted cautiously.

"Well, things have advanced a step or two since then. We know now more or less why he was killed, but it isn't helping matters. In fact, it's making them worse than ever from my point of view. It seems that he was murdered for the sake of a bill of lading he was taking to post —a bill of lading covering ten bales of cotton-piece goods consigned to a certain Ram Dass, of Bombay—and the suggestion is that those ten bales of cotton-piece goods were not what they were represented to be."

"How do you mean?" Blake asked, leaning his back against the mantelpiece and carefully filling his pipe.

"There's been trouble over them in India—a hold-up and another murder. But what affects me is the suggestion that the bales were tampered with in my warehouse."

"By whom?"

"That's what I'm hoping you are going to find out for me, Mr. Blake. The suggestion is that the bales were opened and tampered with while lying in my warehouse, and it's doing my business no good. You know how it is— how easily people get scared. If one lot of stuff, why not another? they say. And that's why I've come to you. I want the thing settled, so does the manufacturer who supplied the original bales—we're both under a cloud as things are now. And with more killings and murders breaking out in India over the stuff—you see what I mean? We're asking you to help us, Mr. Blake."

Blake sucked at his pipe in silence for a few minutes. The proposition was certainly attractive. He had taken a keen interest in the Newman affair right from the start, and tucked away in his own mind he had a fairly complete answer to the mystery. He had guessed quite early on in the affair that those bills of lading would prove to be the hinge upon which everything turned, though why anyone should murder for the sake of a few bales of cotton-piece goods he had not been able to understand.

Now, in the light of what he had just heard, things were already beginning to take better shape. It was not the actual bales that were the trouble, but the fact that the bales had been utilised as conveyances for something else.

"Does anyone know what was actually smuggled into the bales?" he asked.

"No. That's the whole mystery, Mr. Blake."

"But could they be opened in your warehouse?"

"Easily. That's half our business, baling and rebaling goods for shipment."

"And nobody saw them being opened and rebaled?"

"No. But it wouldn't be done when the men were there. If it was done at all, it must have been done at night with the hand presses. On the other hand, our watchman has been with us for over thirty years and swears that nothing ever happened in that warehouse while he was on duty. What's more, I believe him."

Blake nodded thoughtfully. That might or might not be so. Watchmen had been hoodwinked before now. Still, in view of the way in which young Newman had been killed for the sake of a mere bill of lading, it was scarcely likely that the same people would take a chance on the night watchman's silence.

"No," he said aloud, "I'm inclined to agree with you

there, Mr. Tanner. I very much doubt whether the night watchman would know anything."

"Then will you act for us, Mr. Blake? Will you follow those bales out to India and try to lay Newman's murderer by the heels? Catch whoever is responsible, and if possible, bring him back to justice?"

Blake pondered the matter. The job was certainly one after his own heart, and likely to prove worthy his steel. The only trouble was an already over-crowded time-table, but with a little judicious cutting here and there——

"Yes, I'll act for you!" he pronounced with characteristic decision. "I'll leave at once by air, so as to strike while the iron is still warm out there. But first I'll have a word with this watchman of yours—what's his name?"

"Jaggers, Mr. Blake. Tom Jaggers. He's an old soldier, and honest as the day."

"Right." He asked a few more questions, and then, with many expressions of gratitude, the shipper took his leave.

An hour later Blake was knocking at the door of Tanner & Wild's warehouse. It was a dismal enough place, set in a deep court, and approached through dreary, ill-lit side streets.

"Well, I'm blistered!" exclaimed Mr. Jaggers at sight of his visitor. "I thought I reco'nised yer, Mr. Blake. You spoke to me in the office one day—you remember! That affair o' the chap as drownded 'isself out in the basin there."

"So I did!" Blake had forgotten the matter, but now he recalled it perfectly. So this was the man he had interviewed then? Things were going to be easier than he had thought. He looked more closely at the man, noting the honesty of his face and the row of faded medal ribbons on his waistcoat. "I'm looking into the death of young Newman," he said.

"A dirty business, Mr. Blake. A mere kid 'e was!"

"You're right." Blake stood back while the old man closed and locked the door again—evidently he was alive to his responsibilities. "And do you know, Jaggers," he went on when the operation was completed, "I believe that the secret of his death lies in your warehouse."

"Eh?" gasped the other.

"Do you remember the night?"

"The eleventh, warn't it?"

"That's right. And a night or two before that, Jaggers, if you can remember the incident, you had a visitor."

"What? 'Ere?"

"Yes, in the warehouse."

"That I never did!" denied the old man flatly. "Neither then nor any other night, Mr. Blake. I don't allow visitors in 'ere—never nor no 'ow!"

"You're—sure of that?" Blake asked slowly.

"I'm darned sure of it, Mr. Blake!" And when the detective still remained staring at him: "I've never 'ad no one in 'ere nor even left the place by itself since the fust day I came 'ere. And that's many years ago now, Mr. Blake."

"Not once?"

"Not once!"

"How do you manage about food?"

"Ah, I forgot that! My lad brings my supper, Mr. Blake—or used to, till young Newman got scuppered. Then I told 'im to stop at 'ome. It ain't very 'ealthy round 'ere for a youngster, seems to me."

"Maybe you're right," Blake conceded. And then: "Do you reckon to sleep at all while you're on duty?"

"Nary a wink. That's the worst o' these 'ere night jobs."

"Yet you did sleep one night, Jaggers!"

He saw the man's eyes narrow suddenly, then drop to the floor. There was silence for a moment.

"What d'you mean?" Jaggers muttered then.

"Nothing you need to worry about," Blake assured him easily. "Funny things happen to the best of us, Jaggers, and a night or two before young Newman was murdered something happened to you. Does your lad bring you anything to drink, by the way?"

" 'Arf a pint o' mild, Mr. Blake—and the boss knows about that! I ain't doin' nothin' 'e don't know about."

"I know you're not. Don't get jumpy, man! I'm not here to catch you, but to catch the man who killed young Newman. Does your lad bring that beer in a jug?"

"Aye—'e used to—afore young Newman was done in. Now I brings it myself, in a bottle, when I comes on dooty."

Blake smiled. He could see it all now.

"Tell me," he said, "wasn't there one night—some time before Newman's death—when, to your great surprise, you woke up early in the morning and found that you'd slept right through the night?"

Jaggers did not immediately answer, but his jaw dropped. For a moment he regarded the detective as though he were something from another world.

"One morning when you woke up with a nasty taste in your mouth, and perhaps a violent headache?" Blake insisted.

Jaggers gave in then. He nodded his head dazedly.

"But 'ow did you know?" he whispered. " 'Ow did you know?"

"It's true, then?"

"Yes. Yes, Mr. Blake. It 'appened just as you say. The lad brought me my supper and my drop 'o beer, and I 'ad it over there by the stove. And dang me, the next thing I knows is that it's nearly daylight and I bin sound asleep all night! And 'ad I got a fat 'ead? Oh, my gosh!"

"That was a night or two before young Newman was murdered?"

"Three nights afore, Mr. Blake. I remember it exactly. But 'ow did you know? I ain't never breathed a word about it to anybody 'cept the missus, and she told me to keep me mouth shut. She reckoned it were some'at to do with the beer."

"It was, Jaggers! Butyl chloride most likely."

"Bottle—who?"

"Knock-out drops to you, my friend. Something slipped into your beer when your lad wasn't looking. And now, come on, show me round. And don't worry about what you've told me, I promise you I shall not repeat it."

The next half hour Blake spent wandering about the big warehouse. He inspected the hand baling presses and fasteners and realised how easy it would be for an experienced hand to open those ten bales, put in whatever he wanted to put in, rebale and re-fasten them and re-mark them for shipment. Everything he would need was there ready to his hand, for as Tanner had said, baling and rebaling was part and parcel of their everyday business. And given the place to himself with Jaggers lying dead to the world for six solid hours on end—the whole thing would have been child's play.

But the job had been very carefully planned! Everything had been timed to the tick. Whoever had changed over those bales and murdered young Newman had known exactly what he was about. At first glance it would seem to have been an inside job, but in view of the ramifications in India, Blake discounted that theory at once. The affair was too big to take risks on. He had the impression that one hand had done both deeds, and the same hand had collected those bales at the other end in Bombay.

"You ship a lot of stuff to Ram Dass, I see," he said to Jaggers, pointing to perhaps fifty cases stacked in one corner.

"Almost every ship, Mr. Blake. Ram Dass is one of our best customers."

Which explained why the unknown had chosen Ram Dass' bales for his nefarious purpose, Blake thought. Ram Dass would be well known in shipping circles in Bombay, and his freight would go through the customs without let or hindrance. Armed with the correct bill of lading, and representing himself to be Ram Dass' agent, the unknown would be able to collect his ten bales of cotton-piece goods without question. But that rather pointed to a native, he thought. And, curiously enough, a native would fit the garrotting business by which young Newman had met his death.

Was the unknown, then, a native? An Indian?

Suddenly Blake saw how he could check the notion, and check, too, his belief that the same man was responsible for the whole affair. To slip knock-out drops into that jug of beer would necessitate someone stopping the lad. Who had stopped him? And would the lad remember the incident? He might, Blake thought, if the man had been an Indian.

He decided to take a chance, and bright and early the next morning he presented himself at Jaggers' house. Yes, the boy did remember being stopped one night. A black man had stopped him and asked him the way to Fenchurch Street. He had told him where to go, and the fellow had walked with him as far as the warehouse.

"What sort of black man was he?" Blake asked as calmly as he could, but there he remained stuck. The boy could not remember. It had been dark and the man had been tall.

"How tall, sonny? As tall as I?"

The lad would not commit himself. It was obvious to Blake that he really hadn't taken much stock of the fellow. No, he did not think the man had worn a beard, but he might have had a moustache. He wasn't sure. Certainly he was wearing ordinary English clothes, and yes—a bowler hat!

"I remember that fine, Mr. Blake!"

"And how did he speak, son? Ordinary, like you and I, or in broken English?"

"No. He were a proper gent!" the lad said at once.

"You mean——"

"Spoke all lah-de-dah, Mr. Blake. You know—just like the announcers on the wireless."

Blake smiled at that. On second thoughts, however, he

saw that the information might prove of vital value later on. There were many Indians in the world, but not so many with what has become known as an "Oxford accent".

"Did he strike you as being young, or old?" he asked finally. "Was he like me, like your dad, or whom?"

The boy thought for a very long time. He was not as old as his dad because he walked fast and hadn't got bad feet. He was thin, too. Finally he came to the conclusion that the man was like his teacher at school: and upon inquiry Blake learned that Jimmy's teacher was a man of thirty to thirty-three.

Put together, although by no means conclusive, the information was certainly better than nothing. The man who had doped Jaggers' beer was a "black man"—that at least was certain. But there are, of course, varying degrees of blackness. The fellow might have been a negro, or even a dark Italian. He might have been a Spaniard, or a man from the West Indies. On the other hand, seeing that the whole affair was so intimately bound up with India, Blake plumped for a native of India—one of the darker breeds, perhaps, but certainly an Indian. A tall, thin man, probably well dressed and accustomed to wearing a bowler hat. An educated man, possibly an Oxford graduate, and one possessed of some scientific knowledge. An active man of between twenty-five and thirty-five.

It wasn't a bad picture, as Blake saw it. Almost he could envisage the man's face, lean and hawklike, with a firm mouth and cold, merciless eyes. It would need such a man to carry through an affair of this class; to map out everything as coolly as it had been mapped, and to wind up with the murder of a mere boy. He must have spent weeks on the job, watching and calculating and planning—it was surprising that no one had noticed him about the place, but apparently no one had, and it would be useless starting inquiries at this late hour. Far better to start in India where the trail was still hot.

On the way home Blake pondered the matter deeply. If he were right in his ideas the man would lose no time hanging about in England once he was in possession of that bill of lading. His object would be to get to Bombay as quickly as possible so as to be ready to meet the *Indrabrama* when she docked with the ten bales. That argued an immediate departure: and as soon as Blake got back to Baker Street he despatched Tinker to make a few inquiries. First he was to try Imperial Airways, then the Dutch lines, and finally make a tour of the shipping offices. It was then eleven o'clock, and at three in the afternoon Tinker returned jubilant.

He had had no luck with the air people, but an Indian gentleman had left Southampton aboard the *Nuralia*, booked to Bombay, on the afternoon of the 12th. He had signed the passenger list in the name of Mahomet Khan, had travelled first-class, appeared to have plenty of money, was clean shaven, quite dark, tall and thin, was believed to have been wearing a bowler hat, and was certainly an educated man. No other Indian had sailed in the mail boat that week.

"Mahomet Khan, eh?" Blake mused when Tinker told him. "Not much to go on there, I'm afraid—barring the physical likeness. Mahomet Khans are as common in India as James Smiths are over here."

Still, it was a start; and that same evening Blake went down into the city to acquaint Mr. Tanner of developments up to date. He planned to leave the next day for India, and he wanted to know if the shipper had any knowledge of such a man as Jaggers' son had described. Mr. Tanner, however, had not. He had never employed an Indian and to the best of his knowledge never spoken to one.

"There's just one question I'd like to ask you before I go," Blake said, "and it's this. Are you the sole shippers to Ram Dass?"

"Yes, we are his agents over here. His indents are placed through us, and we ship all his goods."

"So that anyone wanting to interfere with goods destined for Ram Dass, of Bombay, would automatically come here?"

"That is so," agreed Mr. Tanner. "Assuming, of course, that they knew of our contract with him."

"I think they would know of that," Blake smiled dryly.

They discussed the affair for a few minutes longer, and then Blake took his leave. There was now nothing further to be done on this side. He caught a bus back to Baker Street, and arriving there was at once handed a cable.

"Came just after you'd gone out," Tinker said.

Blake tore it open.

"Hear you inquiring into Ram Dass affair. Stop. Walk warily. Stop. Please report me immediately you arrive Bombay. Stop. CHRISTIE."

"Who is Christie?" Tinker asked after a long silence.

"Christie, my dear Tinker, is Major Richard Christie, D.S.O. He is also head of the Secret Intelligence Service to the Government of India—and a very sound man."

"But what's the Government of India got to do with the Ram Dass affair?"

Blake reached for his pipe.

"That," he said, "we shall learn when we get there. Have you packed my new automatic?"

"Both of 'em, yes. Why?"

Blake filled up and smoked for a time in silence. His eyes were very bright. Finally he spoke:

"I have the feeling that we shall be engaged in a little shooting before very long, Tinker," he said.

CHAPTER 3

HEADING FOR TROUBLE

A WEEK later, looking bronzed and very fit, Blake and his assistant landed from the 'plane that had brought them from Karachi, and hiring a gharry set out for the office of Major Richard Christie, D.S.O. It was three years since the detective had been in Bombay, but the place had changed scarcely at all. The same old Hornby Road, the same shops, the same heterogeneous conglomeration of faces and costumes—Hindus, Mahomedans, Sikhs, Rajputs, Pathans, Parsees—all the peoples that go to make up the vast Empire of India—nothing was changed.

Blake sighed, contentedly. He loved the heat and the colour of it all. Something primitive in his own make-up seemed instantly to respond to the age-old primitiveness of the people about him. India was still the home of individualism. Here a man could still rise to power aided by nothing more potent than his own right arm and his own personality. Like the rest of the East, it believed implicitly in the old doctrine that might was right—and practised it.

The Intelligence Department had its offices in a large block of buildings out towards Malabar Hill. Blake sent in his card and was admitted at once. He found Major Christie—a short, stiff little man, with greying hair and monocle—looking down on to the road outside.

"Hallo, Blake!" he said, turning swiftly. "That your man you've left outside?"

Blake said that it was.

"Then get him in—unless you want a corpse on your hands."

Blake gave a soundless whistle of surprise. He opened the window and called down to Tinker to come up. Then he turned back to his friend.

"Like that, is it?" he asked quietly.

"That, and more so," Christie replied. He held out his hand, and now Blake saw that something was radically wrong with the man. His face was a dirty yellow. His eyes were tired, and deeply shaded with anxiety. He looked like a man who had not slept for a month.

"You need a rest," Blake said.

"And I'm likely to get it, too, if things go on as they are. A long rest!" The Head of the Secret Intelligence Service drew a finger across his throat, and smiled mirthlessly. "Half a dozen of my best men gone west in a fortnight; and all hell popping on the border. I'm glad you've come, Blake. Take a pew, and let's hear what you know!"

Blake sat down and pulled out his pipe. He filled it, waited for Tinker to come in, lit up, and then gave a brief resume of the happenings in London.

"And you want this Mahomet Khan, eh?" the major asked at the end of it all. He replaced his monocle and reached for the telephone. "Well, there's about two million or so of 'em in India, but on the principle of trying everything once. Give me Police Headquarters, please. I want to speak to Captain Travers. Oh, hallo, Travers? Major Christie here. Now listen! There was an Indian gentleman named Mahomet Khan landed from the *Nuralia* last time she was in from home. He was a saloon passenger, tall, thin, educated, wealthy, and splashed an 'Oxford accent'. Let me know something about him, will you? Yes, as soon as you can. And, I say—go easy. There's a notion abroad that he might be connected with those bales."

"Why the 'go easy'?" Blake asked, as the major rang off.

"Because those bales are hoodoo, my dear chap. The very devil's in the things! If we can find a native who knows anything about them, the next day he's found dead. There's something really big afoot somewhere, but we can't find out what it is. But this we do know: it all started on the day when somebody took delivery of ten bales of cotton-piece goods consigned to Ram Dass, of Bombay, by Tanner & Wild, of London. There was something in those bales, Blake, that has literally set the border afire from one end to the other, and none of us can find out what it is. We've thought of everything—dope, money, arms, ammunition, jewels, dynamite, propaganda, live men, dead men, plague germs—we've gone crazy over the affair. But nothing fits."

"What has happened, exactly?"

The major smoothed back his greying hair.

"Nothing," he said a bit helplessly. "Nothing—and everything! Nothing that you can put your finger on, yet a dozen things that are unmistakable signs and portents. There is something stirring right deep down at the very heart of things, and the key to it all lies in those ten bales of cotton-piece goods consigned to Ram Dass."

"Is Ram Dass himself all right?"

"Sound as a bell, my dear chap. Ram Dass was merely utilised. It's the man who collected 'em that we want to see."

"That'll be Mahomet Khan," Blake smiled, "if I'm right in my deductions."

"Maybe. Actually it was an ordinary coolie, as far as we can discover. He arrived with his bullock carts, presented the bill of lading, and was given the bales without question. They thought he was from Ram Dass, of course—why not?"

"Mahomet Khan in disguise," Blake insisted. "Did he sign for them?"

"With his thumb-print, in the ordinary way of coolies—and then stole the paper! At least, someone stole it from the Customs' file. It wasn't there when we went to investigate."

"That was some time afterwards, of course?"

"About a fortnight. The balloon went up at Famipur; then there was all the trouble with Ram Dass, the cabling and so forth—yes, it must have been quite a fortnight before we worked round to inspecting the actual receipt."

"You couldn't trace the person who put them on the rails?"

"No. We tried till we were sick. The ten bales were delivered at the station in the ordinary course of business, were consigned to Peshawar station to the order of Ram Dass, and that was that! The transaction was merely one of a hundred such items—not outstanding in any way. No one can remember a thing about it."

Blake gave an audible sigh. That was the worst of working in a native country: they never remembered anything.

"Well, what happened then?"

The major released his monocle and sat back in his chair.

"The next thing was news of the dacoity. We heard that a truck train had been derailed and looted in the Famipur District. The local district superintendent of police went out to investigate, and found that the rails had been unbolted, the engine ditched, the guard shot dead, the driver and fireman kidnapped, and one truck looted and burnt. Incidentally, neither driver not fireman has been seen since. Well, poking about, the D.S.P. came upon the wrappings of several bales. He advised Bombay, and in due course the bales were traced to Ram Dass, but Ram Dass denied all knowledge of them. The Customs, however, were able to prove delivery to Ram Dass; whereupon Ram Dass cabled his shippers in London to know what the dickens they were doing. They cabled back that the bales had been duly shipped to him, together with the bill of lading, and that if he himself had not taken delivery, the fault was his. Ram Dass then applied to the police: but when we went round to impound the receipt for the bales—lo and behold, the receipt had disappeared from the files, as I've told you. That was not so good. We thought Ram Dass was playing the fool. We made a few inquiries in London—and then, for the first time, we heard of the mystery of the murdered shipping clerk."

"And that altered the complexion of things, eh?"

"That set us guessing," Christie agreed. "We began to sit up and take notice, and then—" he paused for a moment and his eyes darkened, "then things began to happen. We suddenly found that all our usual channels of information had become suddenly and solidly sealed against us. And the agents who tried to penetrate the screen never came back. Already I've lost six of my most valuable men, and they've even taken a pot at me. They'll try for you, too, once they know what you're here for."

Blake glanced at Tinker, who grinned back at him broadly. That was something they both understood, and had come prepared against.

Then Tinker put a question that was trembling on Blake's own lips.

"Wasn't that train-wrecking a risky business, sir—if the stuff was so very valuable?"

The major shook his head.

"It was a carefully planned and cleverly executed raid," he said. "The spot selected was scarcely fifty miles from the Pathan border—the nearest the line ever goes. It loops round at Famipur, to avoid the Indus, and they derailed the train plumb at the top of the loop. Had the stuff gone on to Peshawar they'd have been up against getting it through the Khyber Pass—an impossible task. But by taking possession of it where they did, they had only to race back over fifty miles of uninhabited desert, and there they were on the border!"

"Then the stuff's gone!" Blake cried.

"No, it hasn't gone," the other contradicted. "That's the only bright spot in the whole ghastly affair. You see, when the train failed to arrive at the Indus bridge, six or seven miles farther on, the signalman there 'phoned through to Famipur. The stationmaster at Famipur ran out on his trolley, found the wreckage and the shot guard, tapped the wires back to the station, and the station called the police. The D.S.P. at Famipur is an ex-cavalry officer, and like a shot he 'phoned his post on the border to look out for dacoits. That post 'phoned the others, and

B

within an hour of getting the information, the whole frontier in that district was closed like a trap. Now, even on the best of camels, it would have taken the dacoits at least three and a half hours to make the border—and they never made it. They saw the helios winking, and stayed where they were."

For the first time, the major smiled.

"After that," he said, "they never got a chance. We've got the border held in such a fashion now that not even a mouse could cross it, let alone a party of gun-runners."

"What makes you so sure that it's guns?" Blake asked after a moment's silence.

"I'm speaking generally, Blake—because guns are the only things out here that amount to anything. Actually it was not guns—couldn't have been! Those bales wouldn't have held more than fifty rifles at the very outside—and fifty rifles isn't going to cause a riot, even along the border. Nor would a few cases of ammunition."

"What about machine-guns?" Tinker asked.

The major smiled for the second time.

"We even thought of those," he said, "but the weights of the bales precluded them."

"Besides," put in Blake thoughtfully, "neither machine-guns nor rifles could have been handled at the other end. Whatever went into those bales was something small and easily carried. It was a one-man job, and not even Mahomet Khan could have strolled through the city carrying forty rifles or half a dozen machine-guns. Besides, where would he get them from?"

There was a knock at the door and a chuprassi entered.

"Captain Travers sahib, huzoor!" he announced.

The newcomer was dressed in regulation police uniform. He was a big man, thick-set and powerful—but his eyes, Blake noticed when he shook hands, were as tired and lined as Christie's own.

"Glad to meet you, Mr. Blake," he said, in a pleasant voice. "Your reputation is as familiar as your name. We can do with you on this job."

"I hope I shall live up to expectations."

"I expect you will," Travers replied rather charmingly. "And now about this Mahomet Khan merchant. I find that he left the ship and gave orders to be driven to the Majestic Hotel: but he never got there. Nor did his luggage. My men are making inquiries now among the gharry drivers to try to discover which one actually picked him up there—but frankly, I'm not expecting any results."

"Why not?" Blake asked, puzzled.

"Because the man's hoodoo, Mr. Blake. He's as bad as the famous ten bales, it seems. Those who speak of the ten bales, die suddenly. And it looks as though this Mahomet Khan of yours is firmly established in the same category."

"That's interesting," the major said, with more animation than he had shown throughout the whole interview. "Blake here believes him to be the man who murdered that shipping clerk in London. He believes that it was Mahomet Khan who brought over the bill of lading and actually took delivery of the bales at the customs. What's happened about him?"

"Well, sir, when he drove away from the docks that day, one of my men on harbour duty happened to be talking to a friend of his—a chap who works down there, a Pathan. They were standing at the gates when the gharry drove through, and when the Pathan saw who was sitting there he stared. 'Mahomet Khan!' he gasped. Like that! The man looked round, sharply, and signalled the driver to stop. Whereupon the Pathan ran over to him and they whispered together for several minutes. When the Pathan got back to the gate, my man asked him who was the sahib bahadur—the big cheese—he'd been talking to, and the Pathan said: 'A friend of mine. I haven't seen him for a long time. He comes from my village.' And that was that. He wouldn't say any more."

"He'll say more when I get hold of him!" Blake said briskly. This was great news. Here was someone who actually knew Mahomet Khan. Knew where he came

from, and all about the fellow. "Have you sent for him?"
he asked eagerly.

"I can't send for him. He's dead."

"Dead?"

"Sure. That's what I'm telling you. This Mahomet
Khan of yours is as hoodoo as the ten bales. The Pathan
was found dead that very same night in a backstreet of the
bazaar. He'd been strangled."

"How?"

"Usual Pathan fashion—garrotted."

"Does that man of yours know from what village his
Pathan friend came?"

"No," Travers smiled. "I asked him that, but he said
no. As a matter of fact, even if he did know, he wouldn't
tell. News travels fast in the bazaar, and you can't blame
even a policeman if he believes discretion to be the better
part of valour. That man's evidently hoodoo, and to
know anything whatever about him is to know too much!
That Pathan knew too much, and he died. You won't
catch any other native in Bombay knowing even his name
—in spite of the fact that Mahomet Khan is the 'Jones' of
Wales. No, sir!"

"But it lends colour to your theory, Blake," the major
said. "The strangling of that Pathan labourer may be
only a coincidence, but it doesn't look like it—in view of
the other things that have happened. On the face of it,
Mahomet Khan killed the Pathan to silence him——"

"To preserve his identity," Blake agreed. "And that,
in turn, looks as though he might be a wanted man on
this side. Do you know such a man?"

Travers laughed.

"I've got about twenty-five Mahomet Khans in the
jail now," he was beginning facetiously, but Blake brushed
that aside.

"You may have," he said curtly. "But not all of them
are wealthy men, educated in England most like, tall and
thin, as much at home in London as in India here,
and——"

"If we hadn't hanged him eighteen months ago, Blake, I could have put you on to just the man you're describing," the major cut in. "You remember him, Travers? Mahomet Khan, of the border province. The Destroyer of Peace!"

"Who was he?" Blake asked sharply.

Travers laughed again.

"Gosh, yes!" he said. "I remember that one all right! Gun-runner and pirate of the highest order. Kept us jumping in our beds for months."

"He was a Saiyid chief, Blake," the major explained, "who was credited with the ambition of setting up a Saiyid autocracy across the border. Report had it that a vast consignment of arms was being worked up through India to his orders—but just as it is with these bales, no one could put his finger on anything definite. The border was alive with rumours and rumours of rumours—just as it is now. There wasn't a Secret Agent from Bombay to Srinagar who wasn't absolutely convinced that somehow, somewhere, using channels that had never been used before, an enormous consignment of arms was being pushed up through India to the orders of this Mahomet Khan. Things were pretty lively, at the time!"

"And what happened?"

"Nothing," Travers said. "As usual! The military built a new road from Battock to the Afghan border, through Famipur, and established an advance police post there. A dozen regiments were moved up to picket the line, and the poor old border was closed again. But nothing happened. Nothing ever does happen! The scare died down, and everything went on as usual. A cavalry patrol snaffled Mahomet Khan himself one bright morning, and after due trial, he was condemned and hanged for his sins—his old sins. And that was that!"

"Had he got a brother?" Blake asked curiously.

"Heaven knows!" the major smiled. "A round dozen of 'em, like as not. They usually have. But I don't think any of them went to Oxford!"

Blake was silent for a moment, thinking.

"You say that this other scare centred about Famipur?" he asked then.

"The same place. But then, so do all the scares, Blake! Famipur is a centre of border intrigue—always has been and always will be. It's the nearest town of any size to the Pathan border, and it commands the Abbabi Pass. That's the only place one can get across for over a hundred miles east or west, so you can judge of its importance —both strategic and commercial."

"Thanks." Blake knocked out his pipe and rose. Upon his lean, aquiline features was a set determination. "What time does the Bombay Mail leave tonight?" he asked.

"Eighteen-fifty hours, from Victoria Terminus," Travers said. "That's ten to seven by your gold watch and chain. Where are you heading for?"

"Famipur," Blake said.

"What?" gasped the major.

"Famipur," Blake said again. "I want to see Mahomet Khan, Christie, and when last heard of he was wrecking a train near there. On your own showing he hasn't yet crossed the border. Before he does, I want to have a word with him."

The major dropped his eyeglass, fumbled for it, and screwed it in vigorously. But he did not argue the point. He knew Blake of old. If Sexton Blake proposed to go to Famipur, he would go to Famipur—and not all the arguing in the world would stop him. The only proviso he made was that he should take with him the major's own special man.

"You won't like his line of talk," he warned, "but he's as clever as a cartload of dacoits, Blake—and loyal to the core. He generally parades as a wandering fakir, but if I were you, I'd make him act as your bearer—your personal servant. In that capacity he will be able to come to you at any hour of the night or day without arousing suspicion. His only curse is that he will talk English: and he will preface all his remarks with 'as the old hymn says——.' Otherwise he's a perfect jewel. Will you take him?"

"I'll be glad to," Blake said. "Is he here now?"

"No, he's on a job in Poona, but I'll get through to him, and he can meet you farther up the line. Agra, say— that'll do nicely. He can cut across country and meet the Mail when she arrives at Agra Cantonment tomorrow afternoon."

Blake asked the man's name.

"Ali Singh," the major told him. "I'll ask Smithson— that's my man in Poona—to give him a chit to you, and he'll show you his authority, the Gold Eagle of the Intelligence Service. That reminds me—I'll lend you one, too, Blake! It might come in handy if you get into a jam up there. I'll tell you the sign and countersign, too. I've got several agents scattered about the country where you'll be working. Some of 'em aren't much good—but you'll soon sift the wheat from the chaff."

.   .   .   .   .

That evening, at ten minutes to seven o'clock, Sexton Blake and Tinker entered their reserved compartment on the Bombay Mail. Before them lay a journey of fifteen hundred miles—two whole days and nights of it, stuck fast in a tiny compartment—but Blake was in no wise impatient. He had much to think about. There was much in this affair of the ten bales that did not seem to fit at all.

He looked up sharply to a rap on the window. A peon was standing outside holding up a letter.

"From Captain Travers sahib, huzoor!" he said.

Blake took it and tore it open. It was brief and to the point:

"I thought you might like to know that that man of mine I questioned this morning with regard to M.K. has just been fished out of the harbour—dead. He'd been strangled. If, as we suspect, that Pathan was strangled by M.K., don't you think it looks as though the man is still here in Bombay? And how in the world could anyone have known that I was questioning him in that direction? Good luck to you. Keep both eyes lifted, you're already a marked man."

It was signed "George Travers".

Blake read through the note twice. A grim little smile appeared for a moment about his well-cut mouth. Then he tore a leaf from his notebook and wrote:

"Thanks for information. No, I still think my gentleman has gone north, though some of his train may still be here. With regard to your other question—inquire at the telephone exchange. The major 'phoned you what he wanted. You, I expect, 'phoned your sub-station to the same effect. Two and two make four, you know, even in India!"

And he signed it "Sexton Blake".

"Give that to the captain sahib," he said, slipping a couple of annas into the peon's ready palm.

He re-entered his compartment. A minute or two later, amid much whistling and hand-waving, the Bombay Mail pulled out on its long journey to the north.

CHAPTER 4

THE ATTACK ON THE TRAIN

IT was close on dusk, the following afternoon, when Tinker saw the temples of Agra rising mistily from the desert. The Mail was twenty minutes late, and the mercury in Blake's thermometer had already dropped to eighty-seven, indicating that the cool of the evening was at hand. He lowered the wooden sun-shutters and opened the windows, for in spite of the whining fans and the eighty pounds of ice Blake had purchased that morning in Bhopal—now a soggy mass in its sacking—the atmosphere was like a Turkish bath.

The song of the rails was slowing down to an intermittent clicking. Outlying villages flashed past, a level-crossing or two. There was a sigh of compressed air as the brakes were applied, a long-drawn-out shriek from the engine, a flurry of lights—and the great train ground to a standstill in Agra station.

Blake opened the carriage door and stepped down on to the platform. The press was atrocious. The confusion was indescribable. He saw black-bearded Pathans from the frontier, fat little Bengali babus, stately Parsees in their funny little oil-cloth hats, swash-buckling Afghans, purdah'd women by the score. He saw water-carriers rushing about with their goat-skin bags, raucous voiced hawkers of sherbet, cigarettes, fly-encrusted masses of sticky sweetmeats, and, of course, the inevitable chupattis. And everyone was elbowing his way into the crowd and shouting at the top of his voice.

"Agra Cantonment!" bawled the guard, fighting his way along the train and shouting out ceaselessly for the benefit of the native passengers who could not read. "Agra Cantonment! Agra Cantonment!"

Those who wanted to get out fought madly towards the

doors. Those who wanted to get in fought madly to push them back. The English stationmaster looked on with an indifferent eye—they would sort themselves out before the train moved—they always did.

Suddenly Tinker touched Blake's arm. The crowd had spewed up a fakir against the side of the coach next theirs. For a second or two it looked as though the fellow would be pushed down between the coach and the rails, but he recovered himself and with the ease of long practice, got his wooden bowl to the front and began to call loudly for alms.

"Alms! Alms, for the love of Allah!" he whined in the high-pitched voice peculiar to his kind. He was a tallish man, covered from head to foot in the saffron-coloured robe of "holiness", with a red rag round his head which matched exactly the red of his beard—indicating that he had made the pilgrimage to Mecca. His feet were thrust into rope sandals and he was—as is the custom—powdered thickly with the dust of the highway.

Now he was moving slowly from window to window. Occasionally someone would drop a pie in his bowl—it takes twelve to make a penny—but more often the contribution would be a piece of chupatti, the pancake-like bread of the country—torn off and thrown to him as one would throw a bone to a dog.

"Alms! Alms for the love of Allah!" he whined unceasingly.

Blake drew an anna from his pocket, and offered it with a smile. The eyes of the two men met for a moment, and held. The fakir held out his bowl—and there at the bottom of it Blake saw the small Gold Eagle of the Intelligence Service. He dropped his anna on top of it.

"Wire Christie sahib that we have met, huzoor," the fakir whispered, as he grabbed the coin. Then he passed on down the train. "Alms! Alms for the love of Allah!"

"Was it him?" Tinker asked.

"Yes," Blake answered slowly. "Slip over to the telegraph office there, and wire Major Christie that we've caught our connection."

Tinker departed on his mission, and in due course returned. The fakir was by then at the far end of the platform. Presently the guard blew his whistle. The station bell clanged warningly. A native porter drew shut the door of Blake's compartment, but the moment he had passed, Blake opened it again and stood back. The engine shrilled. The ponderous driving rods quivered out amid a cloud of steam, raced, caught again, raced again, and then took up the load. As Blake's coach cleared the end of the platform there was a scramble of saffron-coloured robe on the running-board.

A second later, the dust-covered fakir slipped easily into the compartment and closed the door behind him.

"You left that pretty late," Blake said.

"But as old hymn has it, sahib, 'Better to be late than dead'," smiled the holy man. He held out his bowl, and once again Blake saw the Gold Eagle of the Intelligence Service. "The wind blows loudest in the tallest trees, sahib," the fakir remarked.

"So that the wise man builds his houses in the hollows," Blake answered.

"But when the rains come, sahib?"

"Then the wise man knows himself for a fool."

The fakir nodded.

"Ali Singh, reporting for duty," he said simply. He fumbled beneath his filthy robe and brought out a letter. "From Smithson sahib," he said.

Blake took the envelope and tore it open. It was a note from Smithson, of the Poona Intelligence, to introduce Number 61, Ali Singh, to Mr. Sexton Blake in accordance with instructions received from Major Christie. Having read it, Blake would have torn it up and thrown it through the window, but the fakir caught his arm.

"Many slips apt to occur between cup and swallow, Sexton Blake sahib," he smiled. "I think so." He took the letter and crumpled it into a ball, put it into his bowl and set a match to it. Then he ground the remains into a fine powder and sprinkled it upon the floor. "As old hymn says, sahib. 'Dead men sing no songs.' Splendid!"

Tinker laughed but Blake said nothing. He was remembering Major Christie's warning about Ali Singh's love of speaking English. But the fellow was no fool he saw, in spite of his doggerel tags and mutilated proverbs. His eyes were bright with intelligence, and beneath his coating of white dust he looked wiry and fit.

"Have you really made the pilgrimage?" he asked, touching that red beard.

Ali Singh smiled. His left eyelid drooped wickedly.

"As first-class holy man, sahib," he said, "this person is very fine kettle of boots indeed. Prayers fall from lips like water from spout, as we say. Splendid! As old hymn remarks: 'Fine feathers hide the familiar old bird below', but when I cast off garments of holiness and appear as sahib's bearer, then mark of pilgrimage can disappear or remain—as the sahib wills."

"What do you mean?" Blake asked stolidly.

"See!" the other invited, parting his beard and holding up his chin for inspection.

Blake looked. He leaned nearer—nearer still—and his eyes widened. He was no amateur himself at the art of disguise, but he admitted at once that that beard beat anything he had ever seen in his life. Every single hair of it had been stuck on separately, and with the roots and surrounding skin dyed to the familiar crimson colour, detection was absolutely impossible.

"Let it stay," Blake decided at once. "A quick change might come in useful later on. That's a fine bit of work, Ali Singh."

"We go to Famipur, sahib?"

"Yes."

"Then it is good that the beard remain. I have been to Famipur before, but never with beard. It is good."

He disappeared into the bath-room and closed the door. When he came out again, half an hour later, neither Blake nor Tinker would have recognised him save for that beard. He had discarded the saffron robe and the rope sandals and washed himself from head to foot. Now his head was covered with a beautifully-wound white puggaree, and his body was clothed in a long white tunic that reached almost to his knees.

"Khana tia hai!" he intoned in the accents of a perfectly trained bearer. "Dinner is served!"

"Where did you get those clothes from?" Blake asked.

"Wrapped round the body of holiness, sahib," grinned the ex-fakir.

The Bombay Mail was racing on through the deepening gloom. Sitting there talking, Blake soon discovered that Ali Singh was as well informed on the case as Christie himself. He also learned that there were several bad characters in the native portion of the train—faces Ali Singh had spotted and recognised on his way past the windows with his bowl.

"In opinion of this unworthy one," he said, "better to keep all doors and windows locked at night, sahib."

"We've got this far without any trouble," Blake pointed out.

"But as old hymn says, sahib, 'even longest road he come to a finish'. I think so. In opinion of unworthy self, those faithless ones who have been watching Bombay, are now following famous Sexton Blake sahib to scene of operations. Same like jackals, sahib, following a lion."

"Why?"

"When purpose is made clear to me, sahib, I will speak. At present, can only say that it is so. Suggest much caution, and locking of doors and sun-shutters. Where eye cannot see, knife cannot strike, huzoor."

"On the other hand, Ali Singh," Blake said after a thoughtful pause, "it is often an advantage to see the face of one's enemy. If we could catch but one of the other side——"

"It is as Allah wills," shrugged the ex-fakir piously.

At Delhi, Blake and Tinker left the train to dine in the

station restaurant. They had an hour to wait, and the opportunity was too good to miss.

"Do you think we really have drawn the Bombay stranglers after us, guv'nor?" Tinker asked as he struggled with a goat chop.

Blake shook his head. It was a point he could not as yet decide.

"We shall see what we shall see," he replied, a bit cryptically.

At twenty minutes to ten they were back again in their compartment and bedded down for the night. Blake had the bottom birth on the right, and Ali Singh the bottom berth opposite. Tinker preferred the top berth and was already snoring lustily when the train pulled out of Delhi station. At Ghaziabad Junction Blake pulled the shade over the last lamp and dropped his book. That was just after one in the morning. Soon afterwards he was sleeping easily and knew no more until of a sudden he woke to full consciousness and a prescience of danger.

For a second he lay quite still, listening. The wheels below him were beating out a steady rhythm, and he estimated the Mail's speed to be round about fifty miles an hour. As far as he could see in the dim light, everything in the compartment was perfectly normal. What had awakened him? On the berth above he could hear Tinker snoring the snores of the just, and away on his left, Ali Singh was breathing the deep, regular inhalations of a sleeping man.

Puzzled, he lay staring at the shade above him, and suddenly became aware of the fact that dust motes were dancing thick in the air. That argued a draught, and he looked at the windows—shuttered and closed exactly as he had left them. His eyes went to the door—switched to the opposite door—and stopped there.

It was open. And even as he looked at it, it was opening still further. Someone was out there—and that someone was creeping in! That someone had crawled along the running-board; what's more he had a door key, because Blake himself had locked that door not a couple of hours before.

Blake's right hand moved soundlessly to the automatic beneath his pillow.

"Zut!" came a sharp whisper from his left.

Blake turned. It was Ali Singh. The wily ex-fakir was still breathing deeply and regularly as a man fast asleep, but his eyes were wide open. He, too, was watching that door.

It opened another inch, then another. Blake raised himself noiselessly on his left elbow and levelled his automatic in readiness. It was open some nine inches or so now, but the intruder was still hidden upon the other side.

Then, suddenly as it had opened, it was closed again. Blake sprang from his bed. Ali Singh jumped out, too. But the next second both of them leapt back again with a strangled cry of horror. Just inside the door was a big canvas sack, and from the open mouth of it a flat, squat, triangular head was weaving.

A snake!

Blake fired instinctively. Missed. Fire again. It was impossible to know whether the thing was hit or not. Its head drove along the floor with a dreadful rasping sound; lunged swiftly as a whip-lash towards Blake's bed.

And looped inside an ankle-thick coil of it, was a second!

"Keep clear, sahib!" shouted Ali Singh. He was on his knees on his berth, and in his right hand was a wicked-looking knife, not unlike a Gurkha kukri—broad-bladed and slightly curved. His eyes were fixed on a spot beneath Blake's berth, and the detective saw that great beads of perspiration were standing on his brow.

Suddenly he stiffened. His arm went back. For a second he remained poised, motionless. Then, like a streak of lightning, the great knife left his hand and crashed with a dull thud into the floor.

There was a sickening commotion under Blake's berth.

The strangled hisses sounded almost like a scream in the silence. There was a wild thrashing.

"Did you hit it?" Blake gasped.

"Yes. Look out for the other!"

"There it is!" Tinker shouted suddenly. "Right between you, on the floor there!"

He reached out and snatched back the shade from the light in the roof. The sudden glare dazzled Blake. Then he saw it. The second snake had followed its mate, and was not a yard away from him. It was a cobra—deadliest and most aggressive of all the snakes in India. It was coiled back upon itself and swaying to and fro, head upraised, measuring the length of its strike.

"Shoot, guv'nor!"

"No!" yelled Ali Singh, throwing himself sideways. He was dead in line behind it, and could not move. Even if Blake's bullet struck the snake, it would pass clean through it and bury itself in Ali Singh's body.

Blake saw the danger, and paused. A sudden hiss made it clear the snake was about to strike. It tensed. Its filthy jaws opened wide. But in the split second when its head came forward, Tinker knocked it backwards with a well-aimed pillow.

Quick as lightning, Blake ripped the blankets from his bed and threw them over both snake and pillow. The blankets rose instantly as the snake struck again, but already Ali Singh had slid over the foot of his berth, and snatched up the knife from where it still quivered point downwards in the floor. The blankets heaved obscenely. Suddenly the pillow was thrown clear and the blanket rose in a high arch.

"Allah!" hissed Ali Singh as he struck downwards and severed that arch at a blow. Two gory stumps showed for an instant between the cut blanket; then Ali Singh chopped again.

He was still chopping when lights flashed past the windows. Two minutes later, the Bombay Mail braked to a standstill in Amballa station.

Blake lit a cigarette. The flame was not quite steady as he held it, otherwise there was nothing to show the strain he had laboured under during the past few minutes. He opened the window and leaned out. When the guard came along, he called him.

"Anything wrong, sir?" the man asked, for it was then three o'clock in the morning.

Blake mentioned his name, and showed the man his authority from Major Christie, countersigned by the Inspector-General of Police.

"I want this mess cleared away," he said.

The guard peered into the carriage.

"My God!" he whispered when he realised what that mess was.

"I was taking the things up-country for experimental purposes," Blake said. "Unfortunately, they escaped."

"But you're not supposed to travel with dangerous——"

"I know!" Blake snapped. He tapped the police authority meaningly. "Have it cleared away, guard. And keep your mouth shut!"

"Very good, sir!"

A couple of minutes later, three scared-looking coolies arrived with a bucket of water and brushes. Blake slipped on his dressing-gown, paused to examine that door, and then stepped down on to the platform. Tinker followed him.

"We're going to get some coffee, Ali Singh!" he said in a loud voice. "You look after yourself."

"Bahut atcha, sahib!" returned the pseudo-bearer, doubtless for the benefit of the coolies. "Very good, sir."

"Men I don't mind," said Sexton Blake as he walked towards the refreshment-room. "Animals I don't mind. But when it comes to snakes——"

"Looks as though Ali Singh was right when he said those Bombay stranglers were following us."

"Yes." Blake swallowed his coffee, inwardly blessing the custom by which the khansamahs of railway refreshment-rooms are always on duty. They manage those things better in India than in England. Presently the guard appeared in the doorway. "Time's up, sir!" he said.

"I want one minute, guard. I have to send a telegram," Blake informed him coolly. He added: "Police!"

"Very good, sir."

Blake walked swiftly into the telegraph office. There was only one clerk on duty—a young Hindu. The office was empty.

"Have any telegrams been despatched since the Mail arrived?" he asked. "My name is Sexton Blake. Here is my authority for asking. I have one minute to spare."

The young Hindu was too utterly taken aback to do more than stare. Blake slapped down his authority on the counter, and, without any further question, stalked round the counter.

"Where are they?" he snapped.

"But, sir——"

"You can read, can't you!" Blake thundered. "Read that!" And snatching up his authority he pushed it under the fellow's nose. "Now then! Have any telegrams been despatched since the Mail came in."

"T-two, sir."

"Where are they?"

"H-here, sir." With trembling fingers the clerk removed two forms from a spike. Both were in Urdu. One was to someone in Bombay. The other was addressed to Famipur. Blake turned them over. There was a name on the back of each, but that again was in Urdu.

"Who sent these?" he asked.

"A woman, s-sir!"

"A woman?" Blake paused for a moment. "Are you sure of that?"

"C-certain sure, sir!"

"All right. I'll take both of these with me. Goodnight!" And without stopping to hear the youth's horrified protests, Blake stuffed the two forms into a pocket of his dressing-gown, and went back to his compartment.

The guard blew his whistle. There was a jerking and groaning of couplings. Amballa station slid gently away to the rear as the Mail gathered speed and passed out into the night on the next section of its journey north. Blake lowered the slatted shutters, and locked them. He locked the doors again, and this time told Ali Singh to push some gear against them. Then he sat down and filled his pipe.

"You have no notion who was responsible for that humorous interlude, I suppose?" he asked Ali Singh, when the job was finished.

"Only Allah can see through a carriage door, sahib."

"I appreciate the point," Blake smiled. "Is the method normal in this country?"

"Not in the north, sahib. In the north, every man meet his enemy face to face. But in the south, every man afraid of every other man. The snake is the method of the south."

"Does the north ever employ the south, Ali Singh?"

The native smiled.

"Even the jackal has his uses, sahib," he made answer.

Blake pondered that. There was some reason—as yet unguessed at—why Mahomet Khan was keeping in touch with affairs in Bombay. That must be so, otherwise the whole chain of events became meaningless. Mahomet Khan, at Famipur, had assistants in Bombay—and it was one of those assistants who was responsible for those two snakes just now.

Mahomet Khan had been informed of Blake's arrival, and knew—most probably through someone in the Bombay Telephone Exchange—that his arrival was connected with the murder of young Newman in England. There could be little doubt about it that up on the frontier something had gone wrong with Mahomet Khan's plans. Mahomet Khan was fighting for time to get his stuff across the border before Blake grabbed him for that murder in England. Therefore, at all costs, Blake must be kept out of Famipur.

So far, Blake thought, so good. That fitted perfectly.

But what he could not understand was the absurdity of the man in planning everything so carefully in England and Bombay, only to find himself stymied on the border. That did not make sense. That, surely, would have been his first concern—how to get the stuff across the border? Else why bring the stuff to India at all? Was it reasonable to suppose that a man like Mahomet Khan would risk his life and liberty to bring those ten bales of cotton-piece goods from London to the North-West Frontier, only to find himself unable to get them across the line?

It was not, and Blake knew it. Something had gone wrong somewhere. Something had occurred which had had the effect of throwing out of gear all Mahomet Khan's plans. Maybe the military or the police had changed their disposition while he was away in England. Maybe someone had blundered across his secret route through the mountains, and without appreciating its significance, quietly closed it. That would have had the effect of marooning Mahomet Khan and his contraband in India proper—and in that event, naturally, he would be dead against having Sexton Blake sniffing round his heels while he himself was sweating to find another way of getting through. If that were really the case, then his interest in affairs in Bombay would be quite understandable.

Of one thing Blake was very sure. It was not those "winking helios" that had turned back Mahomet Khan from his goal on the night of the train wreck. The man who had planned that job in Tanner & Wild's warehouse, killed young Newman, and later collected those ten bales of cotton-piece goods from the customs' shed in Bombay, was a better tactician than that!

Mahomet Khan would have known all about the watchman on the Indus bridge, and been able to gauge his potentiality for harm. He would have known, too, that he needed three and a half hours of peace in which to cover that last lap across the desert and get his stuff safely over the border.

If Blake was any judge of a man, Mahomet Khan would

have taken very careful steps to insure that he enjoyed those three and a half hours of uninterrupted peace!

No, he concluded as he knocked out his pipe, something had gone wrong somewhere. Mahomet Khan had been tripped up on the last lap when actually within sight of his goal. The only question was—how, and by what?

Maybe those two telegrams in his pocket might afford some clue, Blake thought as he settled himself down for what remained of the night.

When he awoke again it was broad daylight, and the Mail was approaching Lahore. They breakfasted there, lunched at Lalamusa, took tea at Pindi, and shortly after five o'clock in the evening ran into Battock station. There the party was met by a cheery young officer—one Captain James Winfield by name—who introduced himself as Superintendent of Police for the Famipur District, and host-prospective of the party. He had brought his car to fetch them.

"Pin your liver down, sir!" he advised Blake, as they passed through the station. "She bucks a bit in a seaway."

Blake saw that the car was a fine, fruity old Ford, of pre-war vintage.

CHAPTER 5

ABDUL AZA

Captain James Winfield had joined the Frontier Police from a crack Indian cavalry regiment, and he was still more fighter than thinker. "A good man with his hands, but not of much use with his head" had been the somewhat crude legend appended to one of his earlier Sandhurst reports, and it fitted him exactly. A fine sportsman, open-handed to a fault—there was no mistaking his breed. Everything he did was done in broad daylight and well above board, and his word was his bond. Impatient of intrigue, mistrusting subtlety, he went straight to the heart of everything like a bull at a gate.

He did so now.

"Well, what have you come for?" he asked, when the car had been persuaded to start. "I had a wire from Bombay telling me to meet you and arrange accommodation, but nothing else. Wires cost money, I suppose! Are you on the bale job?"

"Partly that," Blake agreed. "But mainly to apprehend a gentleman by the name of Mahomet Khan who killed a man in England and fled to India. I have the feeling that he is hiding in Famipur, and I want to see him."

"I can offer you a fine selection of Mahomet Khans, Mr. Blake. I've got four constables of that name, as well as——"

"Quite!" Blake smiled. He was getting just a bit tired of that joke. "But this gentleman of mine is no ordinary Mahomet Khan," he explained carefully. "He was educated in England, probably at Oxford, and is a gentleman—under the cloak. Anyhow, he must be a power in his own village, and a well-known man."

"Sure he's still alive?" Winfield asked unexpectedly.

"What do you mean?"

"Well, we hanged just such a chap as you're describing —some little time back."

"You mean the Saiyid chief?"

"That's right. He would have fitted your bill to a T. But I see you know of him already."

Blake nodded.

"The Destroyer of Peace? The gun-runner?"

"That's the chap. What's this specimen of yours been up to?"

"Gun-running. Destroying the peace," Blake said slowly. "Rather funny when you come to think of it."

Winfield laughed.

"If you're thinking that this fellow of yours might be the ghost of that other—pack up on it!" he advised cheerfully. "That other was hanged by a lad of my own regiment, and you can take it from me—although I'm out of it now, worse luck—when the 21st set their hands to a job, they do it. Where's this scout of yours been doing his gun-running performance?"

Blake woke himself from a pleasant day-dream.

"Did I say 'gun-running'?" he asked. "I should have said 'bale-running', I'm sorry. If I'm correct in my reading of the affair, the Mahomet Khan under discussion is the man who tried to run those ten bales here recently."

Winfield almost ditched the car in his astonishment.

"You don't say?"

"I do," Blake smiled.

"Good Lord! Well, if you know that, you know the deuce of a lot more than I know; and it was I who discovered the things. In fact, it was my report to Bombay that sent the balloon up."

"Tell me about it?" Blake invited.

Nothing loth, the D.S.P. waded in, but the tale he had to tell was substantially a repetition of what Blake had already heard from Major Christie. It was more detailed of course, and Winfield told it with gusto, but even so, no fresh facts emerged. He was still talking when the car entered the outskirts of Famipur.

Famipur was no health resort—that much Blake saw at a glance. It was just a large frontier town; a conglomeration of narrow streets and flat-roofed houses dominated by domed Hindu temples, and the spidery minarets of Islam now gilded by the setting sun. Beyond and all around lay the inhospitable desert: a wilderness of sand and scrub, with here and there an isolated, stunted palm tree. Southwards the plain continued to the fat fields of the Punjaub; northwards to the border, where the great bulk of the Himalayas lay like a painted strip against the skyline.

"What do you do here?" Blake asked curiously.

"If you mean me," grinned the D.S.P., "champ the bit and grow old. If you mean the natives, they do what other natives do. They get born, get married, and presently peg out. A hectic life, believe me!"

"You contrive to look well on it!"

"I'm a philosopher, brother." The D.S.P. paused to curse in most unphilosophic language the driver of a bullock cart who was sleeping serenely on top of his load. That accomplished to his entire satisfaction, he swung the car perilously between two broken-down gate-posts, and pulled up outside a long, low, heavily thatched bungalow that might have been a house or a barn.

"Home!" he announced with a grin. "Come into the marble halls, gentlemen, and see how the poor live."

Blake and Tinker followed him inside. The room into which the D.S.P. conducted them was high ceilinged and cool, furnished with native furniture, but eminently comfortable. In the incongruous way of the East, several magnificent Persian rugs were strewn carelessly upon the floor, while the yellow lamplight was reflected from polished brass and odds and ends of silverware. A khitmutghar came in with a bottle of whisky and three glasses. Another brought cheroots and cigars, and a silver lighter—evidently a relic of Winfield's regimental days.

"By the way," Blake asked, when they were alone again. "Can you read Urdu in the native characters?"

"I wouldn't be much use here if I couldn't! What is it you want?"

Blake produced his two telegrams.

"What do those say?" he asked.

The D.S.P. looked at them.

"What are they?" he asked. "Jokes, or something?"

"I don't know. What do they say?"

"Well, this one's addressed to someone named 'Wasran Ali' at a number in the Bombay bazaar. It says:

" 'Father pleased with new son. Baby doing well.'

"And it's signed 'Mother'."

In spite of himself, Blake smiled. Not much there!

"And the other?" he asked.

"That's sent to 'Abdul Aza, Kabul Gate, Famipur,' and it says:

" 'Arriving with owl tomorrow.'

"And it's signed 'Canary'."

There was a moment's silence, then:

"Is 'Canary' a woman's name?" Blake asked.

"In this sense, yes. It means 'Bird of Song'."

"Who is Abdul Aza?"

"A silversmith at the Kabul Gate."

"Know anything about him?"

"Not a great deal, no. He came here from Peshawar a couple of years or so ago. He's a Pathan from over the border."

Blake nodded thoughtfully. According to the Hindu telegraph clerk, both telegrams had been sent by a woman. The first seemed ordinary enough, but the second might be anything.

"Do natives keep owls round here?" he asked.

"They keep anything they can lay their hands on," Winfield shrugged. "But if you ask me anything, the word as it is used there means a person. It may be some-one who is known locally as 'the Wise One'. Where did you get them?"

Blake told him about the snake business, and his visit to the telegraph office.

"What made you think of going there?" the D.S.P. asked curiously.

Again Blake explained.

"There is a tie-up between Mahomet Khan in Famipur and his lieutenants in Bombay," he said. "It struck me that whoever had tried on the snake business would want to inform Mahomet Khan of its failure as early as possible. The train stops for twenty minutes at Amballa—a good opportunity. I walked along the platform so that the interested party would be bound to see me and know that his attempt had failed. Then I went to the telegraph office to see if anything had happened. Those two wires were the only ones that had been despatched, and both had been sent off by a woman."

He paused for a moment.

"If the first wire is what it seems," he said then, "like enough the second is equally innocent. On the other hand, if the second is a code wire of some kind, the first will be the same. Could you get some information about that Wasran Ali man—the Bombay fellow?"

"I'll wire headquarters right away, if you like," Winfield offered. "And if you'd care to have a word with the other chap, Abdul Aza, I can send for him at the same time. You might ask him what the wire means."

"I think I know that already," Blake said with one of his quiet smiles. "The 'owl' is myself. It came to me just now when you mentioned that 'canary' meant 'Bird of Song'. You remember that old nursery rhyme 'Who killed Cock Robin'? Well, what did the owl do?"

"Heaven knows!" the D.S.P. gave up.

"The owl dug the grave, didn't he? 'Who dug his grave? "I", said the owl, "with my little trowel. I dug his grave".' That's how it goes, isn't it?"

"Well?"

"Well, that makes the owl a grave-digger. And a grave-digger is a sexton. And I'm Sexton Blake."

There was a moment's silence, then the D.S.P. let out a roar of laughter.

"By gosh," he cried, "that's good! I'd never have thought of it in a year. It's as plain as a pikestaff, now you mention it. But in that case——"

"In that case," Blake said thoughtfully, "we've at last got our hands on somebody who knows something. This Abdul Aza is either a principal, or at least a man in the plot. Either he is in the know himself, or his shop is used as a clearing-house for messages between Bombay and Famipur. That wire reads now:

" 'Arriving with Sexton Blake tomorrow. Canary.'

And that's the message Abdul Aza has to pass on to Mahomet Khan."

"Why Mahomet Khan?" Winfield asked.

"Because of the thought behind the word. Mahomet Khan was educated in England and would know the old nursery rhymes—and he's about the only man round here who would. It was he who thought of it, I'm certain."

"And the 'canary'?"

"I'm not worrying about that, for the moment. I'm interested in this fellow, Abdul Aza. We must see him at once, Winfield—and in his own place."

"Then you'll have to go as a native—and pretty late, at that! It wouldn't be safe otherwise, unless we took a few police with us, and sight of the police would shut him up at once. Can you speak the lingo?"

"Not well enough for that, I'm afraid," Blake regretted. "I understand it, but I can't speak it well enough to pass as a native."

"Act dumb, then—or stammer badly. You can be a 'foreigner' from down country—that's the idea. I'll make you a Madrassi. You would pass nicely as a Madrassi. We'll start off after dinner."

That settled, the D.S.P. showed Blake and Tinker to their room and left them. Ali Singh had already unpacked their white evening kit and was waiting in correct bearer fashion to help them dress. So far, Blake had not told the D.S.P. of Ali Singh's masquerade—at the fellow's own request. He wanted to be treated as an ordinary servant, since that would allow him greater freedom among the other servants.

Now he helped Blake off with his clothes.

"You know all the tricks!" Blake said with amusement. He went into the bath-room, sluiced himself in the tin tub provided, and then made way for Tinker. When he emerged again, a few minutes later, wrapped from head to foot in a large bath towel, Ali Singh was carefully removing everything from the pockets of Tinker's discarded clothes. And beside him was the dhobi—the washerwoman—collecting those same clothes into a bundle ready to take them away to be laundered.

Blake cursed under his breath when he saw the contents of his own pockets, including those two telegrams, laid out meticulously on the dressing-table. He had not intended Ali Singh to see those telegrams. Not that he distrusted the man, of course, but years of experience had taught him the wisdom of keeping as much as possible to himself. He did not complain when a few minutes later Ali Singh excused himself for the liberty on the grounds of having to do everything as it should be done lest the other servants suspect him: but he did make a mental note to empty his own pockets in future, and to tell Tinker to do the same.

Dinner was served in a small, mosquito-proof room, to the right of the main lounge. Soup, the inevitable chicken, pancakes and mangoes formed the menu; and Winfield kept up a running fire of commentary throughout the meal. For the first time Blake learned of the other white people in the station—a Doctor Kershaw, and his daughter Judy. Doctor Kershaw was in the Research Department of the Indian Medical Service—a pedantic, dry-as-dust old man, who came to life only at mention of his daughter. In the beginning, it seemed, Winfield had done his best to prevent the girl from coming to Famipur, arguing that she would be the only white woman north of Peshawar and a responsibility he could not possibly accept. But the old doctor had soon settled that.

"You don't know my daughter," he had told Winfield cheerfully. "She was born out here and is used to things. She knows the country from A to Z, and understands the native better than you'll ever do, young fellow. She ought really to have been a man. She'd have gone far as a man."

Winfield was quite frank about it all. In the beginning he had wished with all his heart that she had been a man —but now he was not so sure.

"What is the doctor doing here?" Blake asked.

"Studying frontier disease at first hand—plague and

the like," Winfield answered. "He's quite a good fellow, but—well, you know what these scientific johnnies are! From a social angle they're a complete wash-out."

"Which leaves only the girl?" Blake smiled.

Winfield agreed, and expanded on the subject. Blake gathered that she knew too much—a condition which since the world began has always been viewed with distrust by military men. She understood the natives as they understood themselves: an almost indecent state of affairs, to Winfield's mind. She could read them like a book, and they knew it. "You can't throw dust in the eyes of that one!" he had heard local miscreants exclaim bitterly. And from odds and ends let fall by his own men, he had come to appreciate the fact that the natives walked in far greater awe of Judy Kershaw than ever they did of him— or, for that matter, ever had. They could fool him but they could not fool her: that seemed to be the general idea abroad in the district. And since he was the policeman and not she, there were times when he found it a very exasperating position.

"I should like to meet this young lady," Blake said at the end of it all.

"You will, tomorrow," Winfield replied a bit grimly. "She always calls in on her way from riding."

"You mean she—rides alone?"

"Every day! And if you ask me why I allow it, I shall scream! I can't darned well stop her, Blake. That's the plain truth of the matter. That girl does just as she likes— always has, and always will. She'd be a proposition for Mussolini, never mind a miserable D.S.P."

"Don't the natives—well, molest her?"

Winfield laughed.

"Brother, Miss Judy Kershaw is a match for any two natives born. She'd take on a thousand, armed with nothing more than her tongue—and by gosh, she'd beat 'em." He glanced at the clock and rose. "If we're going to take a peep at friend Abdul Aza, we'd better be getting ready," he said. "Is Tinker going?"

"No. Tinker can have an early night in bed," Blake smiled.

"Cigarettes are on the side there," Winfield said, "and cheroots in the box, Tinker. Make yourself at home."

"Thanks," grinned Tinker. "I will."

An hour later a grey-headed, elderly Madrassi and a swaggering young Pathan crept silently from the bungalow and took the long, dusty way into Famipur City. It was a bright moonlight night, with a myriad stars shining and the snow-capped peaks of the Himalayas showing cold and serene against the velvet sky.

CHAPTER 6

A TOUGH SPOT

FAMIPUR city is like any other town in India—a huddle of mud houses split by narrow, winding alleys. But being a frontier town, the houses are one-storey and flat-roofed for fear of earthquakes. There is neither sanitation nor lighting—the alleys themselves serving for one, and oil-lamps and tallow dips for the other. It is a place of deep shadows and foul smells, where, after dark, every man walks with his hand on his knife.

Winfield and Blake made their way swiftly through the narrow alleyways to the Kabul Gate. Soon the metallic tap-tapping of the silversmith's hammer came to their ears, and whispering to Blake to keep silent as far as possible, Winfield strode jauntily forward to the booth. It was a single room open to the street, lit by nothing save the glare from a charcoal brazier and a tallow dip stuck on a block of wood beside the tiny anvil. There were two men inside, talking to the smith while he worked. They were horse-dealers from across the border—big, bearded, swaggering fellows, who looked up insolently at Winfield's entry.

Winfield appeared not to notice them.

"Can the silversmith mend a pistol in haste?" he asked.

Abdul Aza sat back on his heels so that the light from the brazier shone full upon his face. He was a man of middle age, Blake saw, bearded, but pale of complexion. His eyes were set slightly on the slant, Mongolian fashion, and as he looked at him over Winfield's shoulder Blake had the curious impression that he had seen that face somewhere before.

"Allah counselleth patience, brother," he said at last, his black eyes sweeping Winfield in one comprehensive inspection. "Mir Hassan here, an Afridi from Pupal, has a brooch to be mended first."

Winfield took no notice of the hint, but bowing courteously, entered the booth. Blake followed him. Without another word Abdul Aza fell to his hammering again, and presently Winfield began to talk with the horse-dealers in their own tongue—Persian. Suddenly one of the men addressed a question direct to Blake, which Winfield translated into Hindustani. The detective stammered out a halting reply, and instantly the horse-dealers touched their foreheads in sympathy—for in India an affliction of any kind is regarded as the finger of God.

Thereafter they left him in peace, and Blake was able to concentrate on Abdul Aza. Where had he seen those eyes before? Where had he seen that head? He racked his brains for the answer, but none came. Finally he gave it up and fell to inspecting the silverware scattered about the shop.

It was then that his keen eye noticed the cigarette-butt lying on the far side of the smith's bench. Someone had been sitting on that side, it seemed, and had dropped it. But the point that instantly caught Blake's interest was the size of the butt. That cigarette was an English make— the natives' were much thinner. And not one native in a million smokes English cigarettes—firstly, because they are too expensive, and secondly, because they are not strong enough.

Who, then, had been smoking an English cigarette in the shop of Abdul, the silversmith?

Blake considered the problem. It was an established fact that someone had telegraphed Abdul Aza a warning of his arrival in Famipur. Abdul Aza needed that information either for himself, or to pass on to someone else. That someone else must be Mahomet Khan or a close agent of Mahomet Khan—and of all the natives in Famipur and district, Mahomet Khan would be the most likely to smoke English cigarettes. For one thing, he would be used to them; and for another, he could afford them.

Could it be possible that Mahomet Khan himself had been in the shop that night?

Blake warmed to the thought. It was a leap in the dark, but the reasoning was sound. Mahomet Khan had ordered his henchmen to use snakes to prevent Blake's arrival in Famipur. They had tried and failed. Immediately they knew of the failure—at Amballa station—one of them had wired Abdul Aza "Arriving with owl tomorrow". Was not that their way of announcing that Blake was still alive and that their snake attempt had failed? And would not Mahomet Khan be eagerly awaiting such news?

Blake kept his eyes on that butt determined to secure it at the first opportunity. His chance came when the brooch was finished and the two horse-dealers took their departure.

"And now for thy pistol, brother," Abdul Aza said to Winfield. "Quickly, I pray you—for the hour grows late."

Winfield moved up to the seats just vacated by the horse-dealers, but Blake went to the opposite side of the bench, to a place within easy reach of that butt. And when the smith turned round to procure a fresh handful of charcoal for his brazier, Blake leaned down and secured the trifle, tucking it away in his belt.

"My name is Belig Khan, and I come from Peshawar,"

Winfield said suddenly to cover his companion's movement. "Have I not seen thee in the bazaar there, O Abdul Aza?"

The smith's beady black eyes rested momentarily on Winfield's face.

"Maybe," he answered then. "I worked for many years in the City of Roses, brother."

He blew up his brazier and set to work. He heated the metal expertly, took up his hammer, and began to tap with great industry. Winfield watched him in silence, biding his time, his darkened face showing sombre in the glow from the heated charcoal. Tap-tap-tap went the hammer rhythmically. Tap-tap-tap.

Then Winfield struck.

"Has the owl arrived yet, O Abdul Aza?" he asked.

The hammer tapped steadily on. The strokes neither hesitated nor paused. They did not vary in pace by as much as a split-second. Blake shot a lightning glance at Winfield, and the latter smiled. Both men knew that their strategy had failed. Either the smith had been prepared for the question, or Blake was all wrong in his reading of that telegram.

Tap-tap-tap went the hammer evenly. Tap-tap-tap. Nor did the smith make attempt to answer until having thrust the metal into the brazier to re-heat, he considered himself at leisure to gossip.

"Nay, brother," he smiled as he plied his bellows. "My daughter lingers on the road—after the manner of her kind. Neither she nor the promised owl have as yet delighted mine eyes."

Winfield was silent for a moment, then:

"Maybe the owl met with a snake on the way?" he suggested softly.

But the smith remained serenely undisturbed.

"All created things rest easily under the thumb of Allah, the Most Merciful," he observed as he withdrew the metal from the brazier. "It is as it is, brother."

He took up his hammer and once again began to tap

c

expertly at the broken mounting. No question as to why these strangers had asked about his owl: no attempt to explain the matter. The stranger had asked a question and had been duly answered. After the changeless custom of the East there was no more to be said.

Then a strange thing happened. A sudden movement in the doorway caused all three men to look up. How long he had been there neither Blake nor Winfield knew—but framed in the opening was a burly Afridi, armed to the teeth, arrogant, heavily bearded. His eyes were jet black and narrowed to tiny slits. Blake noticed that his right hand was hidden inside his embroidered jacket.

"Peace be with you, O Abdul Aza," he called out in a harsh, grating voice. He looked from Blake to Winfield and back again—questioningly—at the smith. "Is it too late to mend a broken bridle?" he asked then.

Abdul Aza sat back on his heels. He gave two sharp raps on his anvil before once again commencing work on Winfield's pistol.

"Am I the only silversmith in the bazaar?" he asked with well-assumed petulance.

"The only one worthy to work on my bridle!" grumbled the Afridi.

"Then bring me thy bridle tomorrow, brother. I work no more tonight. Must I then work all Allah's hours?"

He gave two sharper, more peremptory taps on the anvil—after the manner of a blacksmith timing his "striker", and after another glance round the shop, the Afridi—still grumbling—turned on his heel and stalked out into the darkness.

No one spoke. Abdul Aza proceeded with his work, and Winfield sat staring at the empty doorway. But now the smith's hammer was moving faster, as though anxious to be done with the job. And presently the pistol was finished.

Winfield rose slowly to his feet, inspected the repair carefully and approved it. From a bag of money in his belt he extracted two rupees which he handed to the smith.

"May Allah watch over thee and guard thee always," he said ceremoniously as he went out.

"And thee, too, brother from the City of Roses," responded the smith easily.

He watched them into the warm darkness of the alley outside. He was still watching them as they turned the corner.

"Watch out for that Afridi behind!" Winfield whispered the moment they were out of earshot. "You were right about Abdul Aza, Blake! He's up to no good."

"What do you mean?"

Winfield waited until they were round the next corner, then he paused.

"That Afridi you saw was none other than the notorious Bir Beg—King of the Border Rifle-Thieves," he said. "And Abdul Aza is working with him. Did you note those taps on the anvil? They were the signal to him to clear off and keep his mouth shut. Abdul Aza was worried about us. He couldn't fathom what we were after."

"He certainly didn't give much away!"

"He had been warned. He was waiting for that question about the owl, and when it came he had his answer ready. I'm sorry I mentioned the snakes, it may have given us away."

"Unless he thought us two of Mahomet Khan's henchmen from Bombay," Blake said slowly. "After all, no one save the actual senders of that wire could possibly have known its contents."

They walked on in silence for a moment, then:

"We shall soon know that," Winfield said a bit grimly. "If he thought us Mahomet Khan's men we shall be safe. If he didn't, we shan't be safe. You are sure no one save ourselves knows that you got those telegrams from the clerk? What about that man of yours?"

"Ali Singh is all right," Blake said. He had suddenly remembered the cigarette-butt he had picked up in the silversmith's shop. If, as he suspected, Mahomet Khan himself had paid a visit to the smith that night—there was the answer to the D.S.P.'s question.

He said as much to Winfield as they walked along through the thick dust.

"Find what store stocks cigarettes of that brand and we'll soon have Mahomet Khan under lock and key. There can't be many shops stocking them, and fewer still natives who smoke them."

"What kind was it? Did you notice the brand?"

"Yes. State Express '555'."

"What?"

"555's," Blake repeated. "I saw the figures distinctly in the glow from the brazier. Why?"

The D.S.P. gave a short little laugh.

"Well, that has torn it!" he said. "There is only one man in Famipur who keeps 555's, and only one man who smokes them——"

"Who's that?" Blake interrupted tensely.

"Me."

"You?"

"I myself, my dear fellow." And as Blake's jaw dropped: "Bit of a set-back, what?" he jibed.

"But you weren't smoking in the shop!" Blake cried. "That butt couldn't have been yours."

"That's true enough. But it came from my bungalow. There are no stores in the bazaar stocking European cigarettes. And there are no tobacconists out here. My cigarettes—like my cheroots, tobacco, food, and everything else—are all imported direct from the big stores in Peshawar."

"Then who could have dropped that one?"

"Most likely one of my servants—they all pinch them! It's what they call the dastur—the custom. On the other hand, I really can't think that any man of mine is in this affair—mainly because none of them knows about that wire. Did that man of yours know about it?"

Blake thought for a moment. Ali Singh had certainly removed the two telegrams from his pocket earlier in the evening, and might—or might not—have read their contents. But it would be ridiculous to suspect Ali Singh.

"I got him on Major Christie's personal recommendation," he said. "And besides, how would he come by one of your cigarettes?"

"Oh, they stick together—these native servants, Blake. My man would entertain him, you know—and like as not make him a present of a handful. It's the dastur, I tell you. Anyway, it's pretty obvious that one of our servants has double-crossed us. One of 'em is working with the hounds and with the hare! And since none of my lads knows anything whatever about the wires—it must be yours!"

"But that's impossible," Blake said slowly. "If Ali Singh were working for Mahomet Khan, why should he have saved my life from Mahomet Khan's snakes? That doesn't make sense, does it? Mahomet Khan wants me dead and out of the way, and his lieutenant goes out of his way to save me! That's silly, isn't it? Moreover, Ali Singh knows that he's going to collect a cool thousand rupees when I lay Mahomet Khan by the heels; so it's in his interests to help, not to hinder."

"All the same, I wouldn't trust him," the D.S.P. insisted. "I wouldn't trust him, Blake. But I'll tell you what—we can at least find out which of them has been into the bazaar tonight. That would give us a line on one of them, anyway!"

"Yes, we might do that," Blake agreed.

They had been walking swiftly yet carefully in the middle of the road, but now, as they approached a bottleneck, Winfield suggested that they increased their pace.

"We don't want to get snaffled in a place like that!" he whispered as the houses closed in on them.

Blake nodded, and they broke into a trot. The houses were scarcely a dozen feet apart, and the alley itself was in deepest gloom. Not a light was showing anywhere. Their footsteps made no sound in the thick dust.

Suddenly Winfield checked in his stride. He glanced over his shoulder and then forward into the shadows.

"We're trapped!" he whispered urgently. "There are men in front of us, and more at the back!" He looked at the silent houses on both sides of him, then down at the dimly discernible doors.

"Look out!" Blake cried tensely.

Three shadowy forms were racing in upon them from the front. Thudding feet behind told their own tale. It was neck or nothing now!

There was no time for science. Swinging round, Blake caught the firstcomer squarely on the point of his bearded jaw, felling him like an ox. The second, who had glinting steel in his hand, Winfield sent down with a flying kick to the stomach. The third, Blake laid flat with a lightning uppercut.

But now the men behind had caught up. There seemed to be a dozen or more of them jammed solid in the narrow alley. Blake lashed out at the nearest, and sent him reeling back upon his fellows.

"Back to this door, Blake!" cried the D.S.P. "Kick it in if you get the chance."

The detective jammed his knee into the stomach of the next comer, and with his free foot back-heeled savagely at the carven door behind him. If they could only crash it in and get inside out of the press, they might yet escape.

But now the mob was closing in. Someone made a wild swipe at Blake with his dagger, but the detective ducked just in time so that only his turban was swept away. The next second, bracing himself against that solid door, Blake drove his foot hard into his assailant's stomach, crippling him horribly. The man fell back with a choking gasp, and behind him, Blake saw the powerful figure of the Afridi who had entered the silversmith's shop —he whom Winfield had named Bir Beg, King of the Border Rifle Thieves. He had a pistol in his hand, and behind it, his white teeth showed bared in the gloom.

For a split second Blake faced that pistol, paralysed. The man was not a yard away, and the pistol was levelled plumb at Blake's face. Blake dropped. It was the onl·⸱

thing he could do. And at the same moment there was a flash and a roar, and a dull thud as the bullet crashed into the door behind him.

Someone yelled, but the yell was his last! For his mouth was still open when the D.S.P.—having possessed himself of someone's sword—literally clove him to the teeth.

Now Blake was on his feet again, and Winfield was sweeping a wide arc round them with his sword. Blake attacked that carven door frantically, but the thing might have been of Bessemer steel for all the impression he could make. Suddenly there was a pistol shot from farther up the alley. Another, and yet another.

"Sirkar ki jai!" roared a voice. "Government for ever!"

It was the police!

Another shot spanged down the narrow alley—a ricochet. Blake and Winfield pressed themselves close as possible to the wall behind—in case of accidents. Still another followed it—wildly, blindly. Two more! Then the attackers broke and fled.

"This way, sahib!" called a voice from the other end of the bottle-neck.

"I'll give that chap a medal, whoever he is!" panted the D.S.P. as they raced off.

"It's Ali Singh, I'm afraid!" smiled Blake.

"So he was in the bazaar, then!"

Blake could have laughed out loud. For a man whose life had just been saved, James Winfield was singularly ungrateful.

They raced up the alley, and presently found Ali Singh mounting guard at a small cross-roads. He was afraid that the marauders had doubled back and round with the intention of taking him in the rear.

"They won't get the chance if we beat it now!" Winfield said. "Come on!"

Off they went again with Winfield in the lead. In a few minutes they were clear of the native city and out on the wide road leading to the police cantonments. Here they met Tinker, armed with two automatics, racing to the rescue. He had heard the shots, he said, and guessed they were in trouble. He had not been able to find Ali Singh.

"No," Blake said. "Fortunately for us, Ali Singh happened to be in the bazaar."

Half an hour later, washed and changed, with his beloved pipe in full blast, Blake came back again to that same point. Neither he nor Winfield had suffered more than superficial cuts and bruises, and, barring a certain soreness here and there, both were pretty much themselves in spite of the alarm and excursions of the night.

"You're absolutely sure it was Bir Beg who fired that pistol?" Winfield asked for the fifth time.

"Positive," Blake said. "And that puts him definitely on the side of Mahomet Khan. We've learnt something for our trouble, at any rate."

Then he turned to Ali Singh.

"How came you to be down the bazaar?" he asked.

The native looked at him for a moment.

"This unworthy one went out to collect news, sahib," he said.

"Where did you go to collect news?"

"To the shop of the silversmith, by Kabul Gate, sahib. He is known as Abdul Aza."

Winfield gasped, but Blake's lean, intelligent face remained absolutely impassive.

"Why did you go there, Ali Singh?"

"To hold speech with him, sahib."

"I know that. But why Abdul Aza in particular?"

Ali Singh stared. He seemed not to understand the question.

"Why Abdul Aza in particular?" Blake asked again.

"Is it possible that the sahib does not know of Abdul Aza?"

"Know what of him?" Blake thundered.

"Sahib, Abdul Aza is chief intelligence agent here."

CHAPTER 7

GUNS AND BALES

It was a full minute before Blake recovered his usual poise. Several times he opened his mouth to say something, but upon each occasion closed it again without pronouncing a word. He was entirely taken aback. Never once had he considered that possibility. He knew, of course, that very few agents knew other agents—until they revealed themselves—and it had never occurred to him to test Abdul Aza.

"What the dickens is this all about, Blake?" the D.S.P. asked at last irritably. "What's all this backstair business? Who is this fellow?"

Ali Singh answered the latter question for himself.

"Normally, very holy bottle of fish indeed, sahib," he announced, with gusto. "Highly educated citizen, sahib —B.A.—failed—of Calcutta University, and master of English tongue, by damn! At present employed as priceless assistant to well-known Sexton Blake sahib, engaged in tracking down unspeakable scoundrel, Mahomet Khan. Which same I do most powerfully, sahib, with all strength; for as old hymn says, whatsoever thy foot find to tread on, walk plenty."

He paused for breath; and, watching him, Blake found himself feeling rather absurd.

"I ought to have mentioned this at first, Winfield," he apologised. "Actually, Ali Singh is Secret Agent No. 61, in the service of the Intelligence Department."

"H'm!" Captain James Winfield got to his feet. He was clearly annoyed at what he considered an unnecessary deception. There is, of course, no connection whatever between the official police and the Secret Service—for obvious reasons—but in this case he might at least have been warned. He said so. He enlarged upon the point.

He had risked his neck for nothing, since all the time Abdul Aza was a secret agent working for the Government. The whole thing was absurd. How could any policeman be expected to run his district efficiently when half the people in it were paid informers to another department?

"I suppose it was you who sent those telegrams?" he shot at Ali Singh.

"What telegrams, sahib?"

"Oh, for Heaven's sake don't tell me there are any more of you buzzing around sending telegrams?"

Ali Singh spread his hands and glanced appealingly at Blake.

"All right," Blake nodded. "Never mind about that now. Tell me what news you heard at the shop of Abdul Aza?"

The agent cleared his throat.

"Good news, sahib," he began in the formal manner of the East. "This worthless one sat cheek by jowl with Abdul Aza and listened with all ears, as we say. There is much talk in the bazaar that Abdul Aza does not understand—being but an ignorant man. Talk of Bir Beg, sahib, and guns——"

"Guns?" Winfield interrupted sharply.

"Much talk of guns, sahib. Talk flowing underground same like submarine river, as we say. And of a holy man, sahib."

"What holy man?"

"The name is not yet spoken, sahib. When it is, this knowledgeable one will hear same and make due report. But gist of all men's talk is the same—to wit, as we say, firstly Bir Beg; secondly guns; and thirdly, a holy man. In opinion of self, Bir Beg is the one big, black horse. Bir Beg now playing deep game, as we say. Though what he play for remains big secret wrapt tight in bosom of that faithless one. I think so."

"And Mahomet Khan?" Blake asked.

"Of Mahomet Khan there is no report, sahib. As yet, in spite of briskest efforts, am unable to discover hiding-place. Mahomet Khan same like ghost, sahib. Flit here, flit there; all very difficult. Only name. Abdul Aza hear of him wrecking the sirkar's train, but no man give real information. Abdul Aza promise ferret out truth. When he does, this knowledgeable one will make instant report of same. Splendid!"

"You know that it was Bir Beg who attacked us tonight?"

"Aie, sahib. I saw you enter Abdul Aza's booth, and I waited. I saw that faithless enter and leave again, and in my heart I know he up to no good, as we say. So I go on in front of you when you leave—making straight all path, as we say. It is regretted that I could not come to assistance earlier. That is all."

"You did very well when you did come, anyhow," Blake smiled. "And we're very much obliged to you, Ali Singh. You were splendid."

"It was nothing, sahib. Just pop off pistol one-two-three. As old hymn says——"

"Never mind about the old hymn!" Winfield cut him short. "Were you smoking my cigarettes tonight in the shop of Abdul Aza, the silversmith?"

For the first time in the interview, Ali Singh showed signs of embarrassment.

"Who shall say, sahib?" he stammered. "Certainly the sahib's bearer did make me present of two-three English cigarettes—for friendship."

Winfield snorted.

"That's what he called it—eh?" And when Blake had finally dismissed the man and the door was closed: "Well, I'm bound to say we've had a fine night for it!" he proclaimed acidly.

Blake said nothing. He could understand the younger man's annoyance, but, all the same, he was glad they had gone down there. The visit had certainly exploded his main theory, but, even so, there was still a thread or two worth clinging to. And chief among those was this newcomer, Bir Beg.

"I'm going to have Tinker watch Abdul Aza's shop," he told the D.S.P. "In spite of what Ali Singh has just told us, I still have the feeling that that shop of his is the pivot about which the whole mystery is revolving. He may, or he may not, be playing up this Bir Beg—I don't know. But we saw what we did see, and what we did see was not too good! Who, precisely, is this Bir Beg?"

"Like enough another secret agent!" jibed Winfield, unable to resist the temptation. "After all, why not? Nobody tells me anything. Maybe my own bearer is a secret agent!"

Blake ignored the sarcasm.

"What do you know about him, anyway?" he asked on a sharper note.

"Not much, save that he was reported at the time to have been mixed up in that old arms scare of two years ago. Rumour had it that Mahomet Khan had taken him into partnership over the deal."

"You remember that scare pretty well, I suppose?"

"Remember it?" Winfield laughed shortly. It was because of that arms scare that he was where he was now! It was because of that arms scare that he had been sent to Famipur in the first instance. It was because of that arms scare that the military had built the new road from Battock to the Afghan border, and the police had established this advanced post.

"Yes, I remember it all right," he said feelingly.

"Did you believe in it—at the time, I mean?"

"Frankly—and unofficially—I did! It seemed to me that the talk was too widespread to be entirely moonshine. I believe that Mahomet Khan really did get a big consignment of arms up through India, and I believe that he actually got them to the frontier—but he was too late. We'd closed the border before the stuff arrived, and when it came to running it across he hadn't a dog's chance. It was then that he is said to have enlisted the help of the best gun-runner of them all—the Afridi, Bir Beg, the chap we saw tonight. But before anything could come of the partnership, we had caught Mahomet Khan and hanged him—and that was that! Bir Beg took fright and bolted back across the border like a shot rabbit; it's only within the last few months that he has dared to be seen on this side. Now he's back in Famipur."

Blake refilled his pipe. He found this ancient history of absorbing interest.

"You've got nothing on the man, I take it?"

"Nothing that we could prove—short of tonight's affair."

"And we'll let that go for a bit. It seems to me that Bir Beg at large is of more use to us than Bir Beg in gaol."

"Why?"

"Because he is the only rabbit in the field, at the moment. I'm after Mahomet Khan, but Mahomet Khan is invisible. On the other hand, there are not wanting signs that Bir Beg and Mahomet Khan are working together towards some common end—and in that event, if we can catch one we shall catch the other."

"You mean that they are both in this bales business?"

"I don't know about that, but it does seem as though their aims have a common apex."

Blake was silent for a moment, thinking. Then:

"Assuming that there was such a consignment of arms as the one you have just mentioned, where would it be now?"

"Where it was then, I suppose!" Winfield opined. "It hasn't been moved, that's certain."

"So that if Bir Beg knew the secret of their hiding-place then, he would know it now? And since his partner is dead, he is the only man who does know it?"

"I suppose he is—yes."

Blake lolled back in his chair.

"That's interesting," he murmured. "Very interesting!"

"Why? How do you mean?" Winfield asked presently.

"Because by the look of it we have these two men faced with an exactly similar proposition. Mahomet Khan is faced with thinking up a way of getting his loot from those bales across the border, and Bir Beg is faced with getting his guns over——"

"What?" gasped the D.S.P. For a moment he was thunderstruck. "You mean to say that Bir Beg is going to try again for that arms dump?"

Blake smiled at his amazement.

"You heard what Ali Singh said just now—about Bir Beg and guns?"

"But good heavens, man——"

"Yes, I know," Blake said slowly. "But in my opinion, your arms dump and my ten bales mystery are one and the same thing. The two are inextricably mixed. Solve one, and you'll solve the other. Mahomet Khan is working the bales, and Bir Beg seems to be working the guns; and they're making common cause to put me out of the way. Mahomet Khan because he knows I am here to arrest him for the murder of young Newman, and Bir Beg because I am somehow or other interfering with his racket. It was not you he tried to shoot tonight, but me. And the only difference between us is that while you have an eye on the arms dump business, I am concerned mainly with the bales affair. But Bir Beg, too, is interested in the bales. And from that state of affairs I deduce the theory that my bales are in the nature of a complement to your arms dump. And the link between the two seems to be Abdul Aza, the silversmith. I wish I could remember where I've seen that man before," he broke off regretfully. "Could you get a dossier on him?"

"I can tomorrow morning, perhaps, from Peshawar."

"I wish you would. In the meantime, we'll have his place watched—you might take the camera down with you when you go, Tinker. A good picture might help me to remember."

CHAPTER 8

THE WATCH ON THE SMITH

THE next morning, through the good offices of a retired constable who lived in the bazaar, Winfield managed to hire a room directly overlooking Abdul Aza's shop. And just after eleven o'clock—completely disguised beneath the voluminous robe of a purdah woman—Tinker took up his position at the shuttered window and prepared himself for a long wait. The purdah robe is at once the easiest and most effective disguise in the world, since it is designed to hide not only the head and face, but also the figure, legs, and even feet of the woman wearing it. It covers one completely from hair to shoes, with only a small latticed slot through which one can see. Moreover, in a Moslem country, no man would even dream of addressing himself to a purdah woman, and so the disguise is doubly impenetrable.

It was a small room in which he found himself, more like a cell than anything. It was perhaps ten feet square, with whitewashed walls and a beaten mud floor. In the centre of the floor was a soot-blackened depression which served as fireplace and cooking-range combined; and alongside one wall was a charpoy, a native rope-bed. There were no other furnishings, nothing in any way conducive to comfort—but the natives of India do not ask for comfort. The only thing they do demand, beyond a bed, is a stout door; and that the room really did possess. It was of rough, unplaned wood an inch thick, ill-fitting, but boasting an enormous wooden bolt which shot home into the solid wall.

Tinker's first job had been to shoot that massive bolt and then to draw the string bed to the window for use as a seat.

The window through which he peered was of the carved

lattice-work variety designed to allow women to see out into the street without themselves being seen. It was ideal for the job he had to do, because the silversmith's shop was directly opposite across the road and not more than ten yards away. Furthermore, being like all bazaar shops, an open booth, the silversmith had only to raise his head to look straight into Tinker's window.

Tinker studied the man carefully as he worked. He was squatting behind his bench, tap-tapping away at what appeared to be a bangle of some kind. His face was in profile—a strong face, heavily bearded, with a straight nose and a trap-like mouth; but although Tinker studied it line by line he had no sensation of having looked upon it before. Maybe it was the big turban, he thought. If he could see the man without his turban, like enough he would appear quite different. Perhaps he would before the day was out, and in that case he would take a photograph of him.

Time passed slowly. Already the temperature was up in the high eighties, and the flies were legion. Tinker scrutinised everyone who passed and everyone who entered the silversmith's shop, but nothing of interest occurred until just before midday, when, in spite of his best efforts, he was beginning to nod in the heat.

Then, suddenly, he was wide awake and on the qui vive, for there was no mistaking the identity of the man who was entering Abdul Aza's shop—a big, burly Afridi, swaggering, arrogant, with a big hooked nose, a fierce-looking black beard, and a young arsenal of weapons thrust into his gaudy waistcloth. He entered jauntily, saluted the silversmith, and promptly sat down on a box beside the anvil.

"Bir Beg!" Tinker whispered, as he kept his eyes glued to the lattice.

Abdul Aza had not looked up at his visitor's greeting, but now he sat back on his heels for a moment and spoke to him. The Afridi answered, and the silversmith spoke again. They were talking fast now, heads close together, but as a man walked past the shop the silversmith seized his hammer and immediately made a pretence of working.

The action spoke for itself, and Tinker made a note of the fact that the two were on highly confidential terms. Also, what they were discussing appeared to be urgent and private. Now the smith was tap-tapping energetically, but the bangle was cold and his strokes were useless. It was bluff, put up to deceive the casual passerby.

Then, from the corner of his eye, Tinker caught sight of another figure, and suddenly his breathing quickened. Ali Singh was out there. Ali Singh, in his old disguise as a holy man. He was wearing the saffron-coloured robe he had worn on Agra station, and in his hand was the same wooden begging-bowl. His feet were encased in dilapidated rope sandals, and just as he had been then, so now he was covered thickly from head to foot with the white dust of the highway.

"Alms!" His voice reached Tinker thinly through the window slats. "Alms, for the love of Allah!"

He thrust his bowl weakly in front of everyone who passed, but few gave to him. Presently he sat down in the road, as though tired. But hearing—apparently for the first time—the tap-tap-tap of the silversmith's hammer, he got up and ventured to the shop door.

"Alms!" he whined.

Abdul Aza looked up from his work, but said nothing. The burly Afridi spat at him, and when that had no effect save to increase his whines, he leapt to his feet and literally kicked him outside into the gutter.

Tinker watched the pair with bated breath. The Afridi's face was dark with rage; looked almost black against his embroidered scarlet jacket. For two pins he would have followed the pseudo-fakir into the street and kicked him again, but by then Ali Singh had got to his feet and shambled away.

One or two people had stopped to stare, but the fierce eyes of the Afridi soon sent them hustling on their way. He squared his shoulders and stalked back to his seat, laughing pridefully in his beard. Watching them, Tinker came to the conclusion that whatever might be the position of Abdul Aza with regard to Ali Singh, the big Afridi had no knowledge of him at all. Those kicks were too real. His fury too genuine. Across the border they have small use for the "snivelling priests" of India.

Tinker sat steadily on, watching while the sun mounted higher and higher into the heavens, and the shadows grew shorter and deeper. Now the shifting, ever-changing crowd was becoming thinner as the heat drove them indoors to gossip—orange turbans nodding close to blue turbans over the communal hookah. Yet still the Afridi lingered on in the shop of Abdul Aza, the silversmith, and still the smith tapped occasionally at his cold metal.

Tinker fell to pondering Ali Singh's purpose in entering the shop at all. Had he wished to overhear what was being said, surely he would have squatted down outside the shop and tried to catch whatever he could? The more Tinker thought of it, the less purpose there seemed in entering the shop with the almost certain knowledge that he would be kicked out immediately. That would serve no useful purpose at all—unless, of course, Ali Singh had been merely testing his disguise.

He wondered if that were the solution. Had Ali Singh been anxious to discover whether or not the Afridi would recognise him beneath his fakir's disguise? But to recognise a man argues pre-knowledge of him. Did the Afridi know Ali Singh as himself?

Tinker debated the point at length. It interested him. When finally the Afridi rose to leave, he reached for his camera and took a shot of him as he was standing full in the brilliant sunlight.

Later on, towards two o'clock, a gaily dressed young spark walked in carrying a silver-mounted saddle. He, too, sat down and gossiped, but his talk was obviously chatter to which the smith paid scant heed. The work, however, was heavier this time, and the brazier was blown to a fierce heat. Soon the gay young spark backed his seat a foot or two and mopped his brow, and even the smith pushed back his turban as though he felt the warmth.

Tinker seized the opportunity to take yet one more picture of the man—this time with an inch or two of his forehead exposed.

Then, towards four o'clock, the man whom Winfield had sent to act as his escort, stopped plumb in front of the window. For a minute or two he stood looking about him casually, then he spoke.

"You hear me, Tinker sahib?" came thinly through the wooden shutters.

"Yes," Tinker whispered back.

"Blake sahib say come. I wait for you on corner."

"Right-ho!"

With a sigh of relief, Tinker gathered up his camera and hid it carefully beneath his purdah robe. Then he opened the door and stepped out into the blinding heat.

CHAPTER 9

A FRESH COMPLICATION

SEXTON Blake had spent the day going over the scene of the train wreck outside Battock station. He had driven himself over in Winfield's old Ford, but a most careful scrutiny of the permanent way and the desert immediately adjoining had provided nothing whatever in the shape of clues. The spot had been carefully chosen for the dacoity, and as Christie said, the train had been derailed plumb at the top of the loop where the metals swung round to avoid the Indus River. From that spot to the actual border was less than fifty miles; in fact, the foothills were clearly visible from the line. But in the direction of the Abbabi Pass—the only possible way through those towering peaks—Famipur lay sprawled as a bulwark between the raiders and their objective.

Had the loot been taken to Famipur? Blake asked himself. Had it been taken into the bazaar and cached somewhere, until such time as it could safely be run over the border? Had that been Mahomet Khan's scheme? In any event, he saw, the stuff would have to have travelled to the pass along the road—it could not possibly have been taken in a bee-line across country, because of the nullahs. The Northern Punjaub is peculiar in that respect. The countryside is flat as the palm of one's hand, but the ground is riven in every direction by deep nullahs—dry river beds—many thirty and forty feet deep, and thirty yards wide with precipitous, crumbling sides. To cross such country on foot is all but impossible save along the recognised trails. For transport—even camel transport— it would be quite impossible.

Therefore, Blake argued, Mahomet Khan must have taken the road. And since the road led past Famipur, and since Famipur was the only town between Battock and the border, Famipur would be the obvious hiding-place for the loot—once he found himself stymied of his immediate objective.

Now he was back again at the bungalow, and Tinker was reporting the results of his day's work.

"You saw no sign of anyone answering to the description of Mahomet Khan?" Blake asked at the end of it all.

"Not a sign, guv'nor."

"But you caught the impression that Ali Singh was trying out his disguise on Bir Beg, the Afridi?"

"I don't know what else he would go into the shop for."

"No." Blake considered the matter. "He was up here on that arms scare business, you know," he reminded Tinker. "Maybe he wanted to make sure that Bir Beg would not recognise him again. Did Abdul Aza know him?"

"I don't think he did—but you can't tell with that one. He sits there tapping away at that anvil—he doesn't miss much!"

Blake smiled.

"You're right!" he said. "Anyway, develop those films and let me have another look at the fellow. If only I could remember where I have seen him before, we might get a direct line on the whole business."

Tinker sped away to his task. And after a few minutes' thoughtful speculation, Blake wandered off to find the D.S.P.

Captain James Winfield was in his office, and looked up sharply at the detective's entry. He had just been speaking on the field telephone to headquarters, and in front of him was a notebook plentifully besprinkled with writing and figures.

"Oh, hallo!" he said. "Any luck?"

Blake shook his head.

"Have you heard anything yet from Bombay about that Wasran Ali man, or Abdul Aza?"

"Not a word."

"Isn't it time we did?"

"More than time. They ought to have answered by midday today. I can't think what's delaying them. I marked both wires 'Urgent'."

"Do your wires go through the local office?" Blake asked thoughtfully.

"There's no other way. Why?"

"In code?"

"No. Ordinary English. Why, what are you getting at?"

"I doubt if they were sent, that's all!"

"But good heavens, man——"

"Or if they went from here, they were stopped in Bombay, my dear fellow. Frankly, I distrust your telephone and telegraph clerks, both here and in Bombay. The whole lot of them have been got at. The line from here to Bombay is in the hands of Mahomet Khan's men —no other explanation fits the circumstances. Christie himself thought so. So do I. So will you, before we are through. Isn't there a purely military service?"

"Only along the frontier."

"They'll alter that, some day!" Blake prophesied.

There was a tap at the mosquito-proof door, and a native sergeant of police entered.

"You sent for me, huzoor?" he asked Winfield.

The D.S.P. nodded.

"There's a bit of a tamasha on tomorrow," he said, reaching for a cigarette from the carved box at his elbow. "There's a man of the Wardaki tribe died somewhere in the bazaar—a fakir of sorts—and his brothers have obtained permission from the Political Department to fetch him home for burial. He's been dying for some time, apparently. Know anything about it?"

"Nay, huzoor!" the sergeant answered.

"Well, he's dead now, anyway! Headquarters have just informed me of the fact, and twelve of his brothers are coming to fetch him." The D.S.P. consulted his notes for a moment. "That's right," he said then, "twelve of them. They are travelling under a political safe-conduct, and are due to cross the border at daybreak. At sunset they must be back again with the body. The usual stipulations, sergeant. They are not to be interfered with in any way, but we've got to assure ourselves that the same men go back at sunset as cross over in the morning. In short, there is to be no interchange of personnel."

"Very good, huzoor!"

"Right. You will take four men with you and ride out along the road to a point from which you can watch the Abbabi Pass. You will wait there until the procession reaches you, take note of the men comprising it, and watch that the same men go back at night. A corporal and four men will perform the same duty on the outskirts of the bazaar. The rest of the men will stand to under Havildar Habimulla Khan in case of trouble. I'm not fond of these religious processions."

"Very good, huzoor!"

"All right. That should be——" He stopped abruptly and leaned forward on his chair. "Drat that girl!" he rapped out so sharply that the sergeant involuntarily backed a pace. "Look at that!"

He jumped to his feet and ran out on to the veranda. Blake followed him, wondering what was amiss. Then he saw.

Silhouetted dimly against the hills was the flying figure of a girl. She was riding furiously, galloping, leaving a thin feather of dust in her wake. So near the border, it struck Blake as being a singularly dangerous proceeding; but, remembering Winfield's remarks about the girl, he refrained from saying so.

"Will the huzoor sign the duty returns?" the sergeant asked presently.

"Yes. Keep an eye on her, Blake, there's a good fellow," the D.S.P. said as he tore his eyes from that flying figure and re-entered his office.

Blake stood for a while, thinking. Then, seeing that she had turned back and was rapidly approaching the bungalow, he followed Winfield into the office.

"She's nearly here now," he told the harassed man. And then: "Did you say this dead man was a fakir of sorts?" he asked.

"Yes. A holy man. Hence all this fuss and bother. Still, it's laid down as part and parcel of the constitution that we never interfere with their religious customs—so there you are! We have to put up with it. Why do you ask?"

A sudden flurry of hoofs outside drew both men's eyes to the veranda. The next moment the door was thrust open from the other side and a girl ran in.

"Oh, I'm sorry!" she apologised, with a swift glance at Blake.

"Mr. Sexton Blake," Winfield introduced the detective a bit grimly. "Blake, this is Miss Judy Kershaw," he said. And he added: "The biggest nuisance round here, bar none!"

"Now, don't be stuffy, policeman." She smiled cheerfully as she took Blake's hand.

Blake gave her a searching glance. There was something, almost pagan, in the perfect poise of her; in her carriage, balance and bearing; in the smooth tan of her face, the untouched scarlet of her lips, the swift, bird-like movements of her limbs, the mockery of her blue eyes.

"Caught any desperate criminals yet, Mr. Blake?" she asked, with a light laugh.

"You are a fool, Judy!" Winfield broke in angrily. "How many times have I asked you not to ride out towards the border when it's getting dusk?"

"But I like riding that way. There are fewer nullahs close to the foothills, and, besides, the border's quiet now."

"The border is never quiet!" he retorted obstinately. "That's the very first lesson in the police book of words. 'The frontier is never quiet, and things are never what they seem.' That's the first thing you learn on joining. Anyway," he added, on a note of satisfaction, "you won't be able to ride out there tomorrow. We've got a tamasha on. A fakir-chap has died in the bazaar, and the politicals have given his brothers safe-conduct to fetch him home for burial. He's a Wardaki from over the border, and they're a hot lot, the Wardaki's. Any little thing they see lying around they're apt to pick up—and I wouldn't like it to be you!"

"Captain Winfield is really afraid for me, you know," she explained to Blake impishly.

"For you, and of you," Winfield admitted with delightful candour. "And for the same reason—namely, that you're quite mad. Nobody but a mad woman would take the risks you take. One doesn't, in the nature of things, expect wisdom in a woman; but you might, at least, listen to the voice of experience——"

"Why, you poor, dear, dumb, unimaginative, stick-in-the-mud policeman!" she laughed in his face. "If age is the price of your particular experience, thank Heaven I'm young!"

"Huh!" Winfield could think of nothing to say to that, he had never been quick at repartee. He watched her slip from the edge of the table and execute a few light steps for his particular benefit, just to emphasise the said youth. Her sharp little teeth gleamed white from between red lips. Her polished riding-boots flickered in the lamplight. She danced across to the mantelpiece and appropriated his pipe and pouch.

"What's the idea?" he asked then.

"You are all to come to dinner with us over at the rest house—daddy said so."

"Oh!" Winfield looked at Blake, and the detective bowed.

"I should like to," he said to Miss Kershaw. "But I have some photographs to examine first."

"Oh, there's plenty of time, Mr. Blake," she told him. "We don't dine until eight."

Blake left them, and went back to see how Tinker was progressing. The films had been developed, and Tinker was just about to start taking prints of them under the watchful eye of Ali Singh.

"Hallo!" Blake said to the agent. "Have you heard anything of interest today?"

"Until very recently, sahib, nothing. Have paid three visits to shop of Abdul Aza, but upon each occasion, as old hymn says, cupboard was bare. Received heavy kick from that faithless one, Bir Beg, otherwise nothing to report until now."

"Why did Bir Beg kick you?"

The agent smiled.

"A godless man, that one, sahib," he said. "I try to find out if he remember me from when I work here before on that arms scare, but even now cannot be sure. Saffron robe, to Bir Beg, same like red rag to cow, as we say. Kick on sight, sahib, and kick hard. One day, perhaps, he pay for that kick!"

Blake thought that extremely likely.

"What is it that you discovered 'recently'?" he asked the man.

"Am not sure if of terrific interest to sahib, but have

discovered destination of telegram received by Abdul Aza yesterday. Information concerning owl was passed on by Abdul Aza to very fat fakir. Abdul Aza maintain that fat fakir—whose name he does not know—is secret agent working between Famipur and small village just over border. But, speaking for self, sahib, I am not sure. No such agent is known to me."

"A fat fakir, eh?" Blake mused. "Is he here now?"

"Apparently not, sahib. According to information received, same has now returned across the border."

Blake determined to hazard a direct question.

"Ali Singh," he asked, "what is your private opinion of Abdul Aza—as an agent, I mean?"

The native hesitated. It was clear that the question was not to his liking.

"It is written, sahib," he said at last, "that still tongue makes wise head—I think so. But, since the sahib asks plain question, this worthless one will endeavour to answer in same style. In opinion, of self, sahib, Abdul Aza not too good. Sometimes I think he have leg in both camps, as we say. Sometimes I think he work for both sides—he being a greedy man with much love of money—but same hard to prove. Certainly I think it best to say little of importance in his shop. I think so."

Blake nodded. That rather went to confirm his own impression of the man. He saw that if the fat fakir from across the border happened to be one of Mahomet Khan's men, his theory about that telegram still held good."

"We're dining out tonight, Tinker," he said, suddenly remembering Miss Kershaw's invitation.

"Better I go to prepare clothes, then!" smiled Ali Singh. He went out into the bedroom, and for a time Blake sat smoking thoughtfully while Tinker went ahead with his work. He was pondering the matter of that dead holy man: wondering if his death were sheer coincidence or perhaps a link in the chain he was trying to forge about Mahomet Khan. He had not forgotten what Ali Singh had said last night about the three topics of conversation in the bazaar—Bir Beg, guns, and a holy man. Was this the holy man referred to?

"How about these, guv'nor?" Tinker asked suddenly.

"Right!" Blake got up and crossed the room. He took up the wet prints one by one and examined them carefully. Tinker's camera was fitted with a telephoto lens so that the features of both Bir Beg and the silversmith were clearer—having been taken in brilliant sunlight—than they had seemed to Blake last night when seen by the glim from a tallow dip.

"Any use?" Tinker asked after a long silence.

Blake shook his head. The picture in his mind was clearing somewhat, but it was still too vague to place. He took the photographs to the lamp, and for several minutes longer stood staring at them, but still the memory eluded him. He transferred his eyes to the darkness outside and concentrated.

Then Tinker had a brain-wave. Taking up the negatives he selected the one in which Abdul Aza had pushed back his turban. Then he found a piece of paper, and cut a hole in such fashion that when he placed it over the negative everything was hidden save the actual features of the man—that is, both beard and turban were obliterated. That done, and using the paper as a shield, he printed another proof—and now he had nothing on his picture save an oval of face containing the eyes, nose, and mouth of the suspected man.

"Look at that?" he invited.

Blake looked—and froze. For a couple of minutes he stared at the thing, and then he smiled.

"Got him?" Tinker asked eagerly.

"Got him!" breathed the detective. "Yes. I know him now. I ran up against him ten years ago in that case I undertook for the French Colonial Government with reference to the supply of arms to the Riffs. A Russian syndicate was supplying machine-guns. And behind that syndicate was a Russian named Paul Verislov."

"And this is the man, guv'nor?"

"The same man," Blake said softly. "Abdul Aza the silversmith and Paul Verislov are one and the same—I'd have had him before this save for his beard, that turban, and his darkened face. I knew I had seen those slanting eyes of his somewhere before. He's from Eastern Russia, I ought to have guessed it. Now he's passing as a Pathan with a dash of Mongolian ancestry—rather neat when you come to think of it. Ali Singh was right just now when he said the man has a leg in both camps."

"So now what?"

Blake smiled.

"Now things begin to move, Tinker. Now we know who supplied Mahomet Khan—the first Mahomet Khan— with the guns that are supposed still to be hidden in that dump. We know now just where Abdul Aza stands. On the one hand he is acting as secret agent to the Intelligence Service, and on the other hand he is supplying arms to the tribes across the border.

"And if he supplied the arms to that first Mahomet Khan," Tinker broke in quickly, "he must know where the dump is now!"

Blake nodded.

"Also where our own Mahomet Khan has hidden what he took from those bales," he said.

"Oughtn't we to see him?"

Blake nodded. The association of Paul Verislov with the affair put a much more serious complexion on those guns. It was not a few rifles he had sold to Mahomet Khan. Not a few pistols or a few old Mausers. Verislov dealt only in one commodity—machine-guns.

"And a few dozen machine-guns—across the border——" he said aloud.

When a few minutes later Blake went in to bath, his face was set and steel-hard. Now he knew what he was up against.

CHAPTER 10

A VITAL MESSAGE

THE resthouse proved to be not quite so big as Winfield's bungalow, but it was very comfortably furnished, and bore everywhere the evidences of a woman's care. Judy Kershaw was not all madcap in spite of the D.S.P.'s opprobrium. She introduced Blake and Tinker to her father—a typical old professor—and soon they were all seated at dinner.

Ali Singh whisked away the plates with a deftness that was astounding considering his purely amateur status. In India, no matter where one may dine, it is the custom for every man to take his own servant to wait on him. Blake, whose general knowledge was extraordinary, engaged the doctor in a highly technical discussion on plague, and they were still arguing the matter when a servant stole up quietly behind Judy's chair and spoke to her.

"Someone wants to see you, Jimmy," she said to Winfield. "Your havildar is outside asking for you. I've told him to come in."

The havildar appeared in the doorway as she spoke. He seemed agitated.

"Fazl Das is here, huzoor," he reported. "He craves immediate audience."

"Fazl Das?" Winfield repeated. He looked at Judy for permission. "Bring him in, havildar," he said then.

The corporal came in smartly. He cleared his throat.

"This party that is coming across tomorrow, huzoor," he began breathlessly. "I have seen it."

"Well?"

"It is no ordinary funeral party, huzoor. Every man of it is well known to you. Badmarshes huzoor. Cut-throats. Rifle-thieves. I saw them before the sun sank, and in the early darkness I crept up to where they were waiting to cross at daybreak tomorrow. I crept even to their fires, huzoor, and the talk was of guns. Guns, huzoor! And Bir Beg! And Mahomet Khan——"

"Mahomet Khan?" Blake snapped.

"Aie, huzoor. He whom the sirkar hanged. He who had the arms dump."

"Oh, that one? Yes, go on!"

"It is of that arms dump I would speak, huzoor."

Winfield was on his feet now. He shot Blake a triumphant glance.

"Go on!" he urged the corporal. "Go on, man!"

The corporal gathered himself together visibly. He was not insensible of the consternation he was producing among the sahib-log.

"The arms dump, huzoor," he said again. "Tonight I heard strange talk round that fire—dark talk—talk I could not understand. But all the time they were repeating and repeating yet again the one word 'arms'. 'Arms', they were saying "Arms, arms, arms!' And Famipur, huzoor. And Mahomet Khan, huzoor. And Bir Beg."

"Go on!" Winfield whispered.

"And I thought to myself, huzoor, those two faithless ones were in partnership over that arms dump. It was common talk at the time. And now that Mahomet Khan is dead, that leaves only Bir Beg. Bir Beg, I thought to myself, knows where the arms dump is; and Bir Beg is here in Famipur, huzoor! I ask myself, why? Does Bir Beg—dacoit, thief, gun-runner, cut throat!—does Bir Beg care about any holy man living? He does not, huzoor! Then why should he care for one dead? Why should Bir Beg collect a funeral party—this party of cut-throats who can talk of nothing save arms?"

The inference was too obvious to miss. Winfield grabbed it whole—hook, line and sinker!

"They're coming down for the arms, Blake!" he cried hoarsely. "Just as you said. Bir Beg is proposing to open that old arms dump. He's proposing to run the stuff across the border right under our very noses—and, like enough, run the contents of those bales at the same time. But how—how? That's the question——"

He stopped dead, and his jaw dropped foolishly. From Blake's amused face he looked at the corporal.

"Great Shiv!" he half-gasped then. "The catafalque! The catafalque they'll bring down for the body. We've got 'em, Blake! We've got 'em cold! Don't you see, they're planning to open up the dump and hide the arms in the catafalque!"

"Aie, huzoor!" chimed in the corporal boldly. "That is the thought that came to me as I lay out on the hillside yonder. It is a very big catafalque, huzoor. Far bigger than they usually bring."

"Didn't I tell you?" Winfield laughed a bit hysterically. "By heck, Blake, the cunning of 'em! You see their idea? That party has safe conduct to fetch the body of this holy man from Famipur and take it across the border for burial. No one can interfere with them. The actual catafalque is sacrosanct because of the Mohammedan dead inside it. And, in this case, doubly sacrosanct, because they say the man is a Saiyid—that is, a direct descendant of the Khalifa Ali, and, therefore, in the eyes of his co-religionists, a Prince of the Blood. If I touched the thing, the Mohammedans of Famipur would rise like one man and crucify me! I can't touch it, by law. Nobody can touch it, let alone open it to check over its contents.

"So what do they do? They fill the thing with rifles, bung the dead man on top, and walk the whole contraption clean out of the country without anyone being able to say yea or nay! Clean out of the country—and no one can say a word! You follow me?"

Blake nodded. His face was extraordinarily thoughtful. Suddenly he turned to the corporal who had brought this astounding news.

"You say that you saw those men?" he asked. "Can you describe their leader?"

"Aie, huzoor!" the man answered eagerly. "Him I saw several times. He is a fat fakir, huzoor. Very fat."

"A very fat fakir, eh?" Blake asked softly. That was significant. It was a fat fakir who had collected from Abdul Aza the telegram message about the "owl". If that fat fakir should chance to be Mahomet Khan's lieutenant——

"Did you hear his name?" he asked the corporal sharply.

"Nay, huzoor."

There was a moment's silence; then:

"If that's settled," Dr. Kershaw said in his faintly irritable fashion, "couldn't we get on with our dinner, please?"

Winfield laughed.

"Dinner?" he echoed. "There's no more dinner for me, doctor! Apologies and all that, Judy—but I must go. I have work to do. This looks like being the biggest chance of my career. Are you coming, Blake?"

Rather unexpectedly, Blake shook his head.

"After dinner will be plenty soon enough," he said.

"As you like." The D.S.P. clattered out of the room. They listened to his footsteps as he almost fell down the veranda steps in his haste.

"A somewhat impetuous young man, I fear," sighed Dr. Kershaw, as he prepared to get on with his neglected dinner. "Apt to jump to conclusions."

"How do you mean?" Blake asked.

"It's a trap," Judy said flatly. "And if he isn't careful he's going to walk straight into it, Mr. Blake. If those men are really coming down to open that old arms dump, they wouldn't sit up there shouting about it. That corporal repeated what he was meant to repeat. He heard what he was intended to hear. He told the D.S.P. exactly what those men wanted the D.S.P. to know; and now the D.S.P. is going to act precisely as they want him to act."

"Meaning?" Blake asked again.

"They want him to look into that catafalque, Mr. Blake. It sticks out a mile! As you saw for yourself, that is precisely and exactly what he is going to do!"

Blake nodded. It certainly looked like it.

For the remainder of the meal he was strangely thoughtful.

CHAPTER 11

BLAKE FORCES THE PACE

It was close on eleven o'clock when Blake and Tinker—preceded by Ali Singh carrying a hurricane-lamp—got back to the D.S.P.'s bungalow. Just as they entered the compound, Ali Singh paused to point out several tiny pin-points of light that seemed to be hanging 'twixt earth and sky, miles and miles away.

"The watch-fires of those faithless ones, sahib," he said. "They sleep in the hills until morning. Tomorrow we shall see what we shall see."

There was a quaintly prophetic note in the man's voice that caught Blake's attention.

"You heard what the mem-sahib said, Ali Singh?" he asked him. "What is your opinion of that corporal's message?"

"Who can say, sahib? The mem-sahib make one guess, I make another. But, as the old hymn says: 'No one can count pussies before hatched'."

"Yet if that fat fakir the corporal spoke of should happen to be the man who received that message through Abdul Aza—if he should chance to be one of Mahomet Khan's men——" Blake mused.

"Then, sahib—trap or no trap—I think it good to take peep into that catafalque. I think so. Maybe we find what we seek. The sahib will need me again tonight?" he broke off as they reached the bungalow.

"Not tonight," Blake said. "But keep handy, in case anything should happen."

The native touched his turban and went off to his own quarters. Blake and Tinker went in search of the D.S.P.

They found him in his office.

"Well, things are moving already!" he greeted them. "They have cut the telephone-wire between here and

D

Battock, and that's isolated me from headquarters. See the game, man? They think I'll be afraid to act without the necessary authority—but that's where they're wrong. I shall act all right—authority or no authority!"

Blake nodded. He could see that much for himself. Winfield would look into that catafalque tomorrow, if it were the last thing he ever did.

"Do you want to come with me, Blake?" he asked suddenly.

The detective shook his head. If it were part and parcel of the gun-runners' plot to have the D.S.P. look into their catafalque, let him look! But he must do it alone. There was no point in both of them falling into the same trap. If the D.S.P. fell, Blake would at least know where he was, and be able to rescue him. Moreover, if the D.S.P. took the bait they were dangling in front of him, it meant that things would happen. And that was what Blake wanted; he wanted the other side to make a move. As things were now, with everyone standing still and marking time, it was impossible to discover anything at all.

"But I'd like you to fix me up again as a Madrassi," he said. "I'm going down the bazaar. No, you needn't come with me this time—I'm taking Tinker. And I'd like him fixed in something less cumbersome than a purdah robe. It's dark now, and we needn't be too particular. Can you manage that?"

"I can—if you insist. But I don't much like you going down there alone. On the other hand, I daren't leave here as things are now. You can see that for yourself."

"Don't worry," Blake smiled. "We shall be all right!"

Half an hour later, with Blake in his old disguise as an elderly Madrassi, and Tinker got up as a gay young Afghan blade, the two said goodnight to Winfield and took the road to the bazaar.

"Abdul Aza?" Tinker asked as they walked along.

"Abdul Aza," Blake agreed. "For if anyone holds the key to all this mystery, that man is Abdul Aza. And tonight, Tinker, he's going to talk."

Tinker fingered the automatic beneath his embroidered jacket and grinned happily. Things were moving to a crisis at last.

The moon had not yet risen from behind the grim bulk of the Himalayas, and the narrow alleys of the bazaar were almost pitch dark, but the two made good progress and soon found themselves nearing the Kabul Gate.

"You work late, brother," Blake said in his halting Hindustani as he entered the shop of the silversmith. "Is thy hammer never silent? I bring thee a bangle to mend."

"Then will I attend to it in the morning!" the smith answered surlily.

Blake sat down. Tinker took the seat opposite.

"The wind blows loudest in the tallest trees, Abdul Aza," Blake said quietly.

The smith stiffened and straightway went on with his tapping.

"So that the wise man builds his house in the hollows," he made answer.

"But when the rains come?"

"Then the wise man knows himself for a fool. May I see thy bangle, brother?"

Blake produced his Gold Eagle of the Intelligence Service, and laid it on the smith's anvil. Immediately Abdul Aza reached into a drawer beneath his bench and produced a similar token.

"What seekest thou?" he asked.

"Mahomet Khan," Blake answered bluntly.

The smith blew up his brazier so that its lurid light fell upon the three faces gathered closely about the anvil. He looked keenly at both his visitors; and, catching the man's eyes, Blake knew he had made no mistake. The silversmith was Paul Verislov—ten years older than when he had seen him last, and very much changed by his beard and dress and manner of living, but still Paul Verislov.

"I have no word of Mahomet Khan," he said after a

short silence. "He cometh like a shadow and departeth the same way. Who can trap a shadow, brother?"

"I seek, too, an answer to the riddle of the ten bales," Blake said.

"Many men seek that same answer, brother; but who can speak?"

"You can," Blake said softly in English.

The man threw him a startled glance.

"You can—Paul Verislov!"

The smith had picked up his hammer again; but at mention of his name the hammer stopped dead in midair. For a full minute he sat motionless, rigid, as though carved in stone. Then with a noisy clatter, the hammer fell of its own volition on to the anvil.

"Who are you?" he got out at last, his voice a mere thread of sound in the silence.

The detective looked straight into those slanting, Mongolian eyes.

"Sexton Blake," he said. "And keep that hammer going, Verislov!" he cautioned a split second later. "Don't attempt to signal your friends, or you are a dead man. I've got you covered where you sit!"

The hammer began to move automatically; but now its head was falling anywhere. Hardened plotter as he was, Blake's sudden accusation had shaken him to the core. He was sweating copiously, and his teeth were bared above his beard.

"What do you want of me?" he snarled.

"Information, Verislov! Not particularly about your own affairs, but about the affairs of Mahomet Khan. I want him for murder. What's more I mean to get him!"

"I have no information about the man."

"Oh, yes, you have! Just where you stand with the Intelligence Service out here I have yet to fathom, but I know that you are working with Bir Beg—and I know that Bir Beg and Mahomet Khan are working this bale business between them—or aren't they?" he asked swiftly, surprised into the question by something he saw in those cunning, slanting eyes.

There's was a moment's silence. A moment in which Blake's thoughts were working frantically. He was on the wrong track! He had been on the wrong track all along. That sudden flicker in Verislov's eyes had told him as much—had given him the clue.

"So Mahomet Khan and Bir Beg are not working the bales business together?" he asked softly. That put a different complexion on the affair. If they were not working together in the deal, like as not they were——

Blake stopped. An amazing idea had flashed across his mind. Could it be that the two were at cross-purposes over those bales? Had Bir Beg cut in across Mahomet Khan's deal? That would certainly explain Mahomet Khan's failure to get his loot across the border; but, in that event, where did Verislov come in?

He eyed the man thoughtfully for a moment.

"Where is Mahomet Khan now?" he asked at length.

"I don't know. Nobody knows."

"Yet you are acting as clearing-house for messages between Mahomet Khan and his lieutenants!"

Verislov started bolt upright. He searched Blake's face with narrowed eyes.

"What's that?" he asked at last.

He was taken aback, frightened. The detective's statement had come as a shock to him. He was plainly bewildered.

"You are acting as clearing-house for messages between Mahomet Khan and his lieutenants," Blake repeated carefully. "You passed on a message only yesterday to a fat fakir who called upon you."

The Russian gave a short laugh. He breathed again. He made no pretence to hide his relief.

"You're crazy!" he said, with a touch of contempt. "That fat fakir is a Government agent. I have known him for some time. He comes from over the border."

And when Blake said nothing: "I, too, am employed by the Government," he mentioned.

Blake remained silent. He was thinking. Verislov had shown unmistakable fear when confronted with the possibility that he might unwittingly have been dealing with one of Mahomet Khan's lieutenants. Why? Could it be possible that he was not dealing with Mahomet Khan, after all? Could it be possible that he was dealing only with Bir Beg? In any event, if the fat fakir were indeed one of Mahomet Khan's men, Blake was certain that Verislov did not know of it. Verislov had not, therefore knowingly passed on information to Mahomet Khan's lieutenants. And, after all, if the two were not running in double harness——

"I know you are employed by the Government," Blake went on thoughtfully. "But does the Government know your history? Do they know that you are wanted by half the governments of Europe for gun-running? Do they know there's a rope waiting for you in the hands of the French Colonial Government for your work in the Riff country, ten years ago? Oh, yes!" as the Russian ripped out a vicious oath. "I've got you taped, Paul Verislov— quite apart from this present trouble. I could have you deported in chains tomorrow—and I may do, yet, unless you come over with the truth! It was you who supplied those arms to the first Mahomet Khan—the one who was hanged! It was you who hid them when you heard of his death." He thrust his automatic hard against the man's ribs. "Where are those arms now, Verislov?"

"Where you'll never find them!" the Russian laughed shortly.

"I wouldn't be too sure of that, if I were you, Veris- lov," Blake smiled in his turn. "You'll talk all right when you appreciate the alternative."

"Death doesn't frighten me!"

"I know it doesn't. It never did. People in your line of business cannot afford to fear death. But I know what does frighten you, Verislov. You dread losing your liberty. Have you ever seen the inside of a native prison?"

"And never shall! I am a Russian subject: a Soviet citizen."

"Don't you believe it, my friend. You are Abdul Aza, a Pathan silversmith. You are a native now, and I'll watch you suffer as such. I could put you in gaol tonight —here in Famipur. Whether I do or not depends entirely upon yourself."

The Russian saw that Blake meant it, and cooled down.

"What do you want to know?" he asked at last, his voice as thin as a reed in the silence.

"Where are those arms now?" Blake repeated.

Verislov looked at him and his lips curled.

The next moment he shocked Blake to the core.

"Do you really think I'd be sitting here tapping at native silver if I could tell you that?" he asked.

Blake forced himself to give no sign.

"Yet you hid them!" he accused the man.

"That's true. But they didn't stay hid!"

"You mean that somebody stole them?"

"I don't suppose they walked away."

"No." Blake ignored the sarcasm. Only with the greatest difficulty could he keep his hands off that mocking mouth. "Who does know where they are?" he asked coolly.

The Russian grated his teeth.

"The swine you want for murder," he rasped out viciously. "Mahomet Khan—may his soul rest in hell!"

So that was it! Blake saw, now, where he had gone wrong. Mahomet Khan had stolen Verislov's guns from their hiding-place, and Verislov had now linked up with Bir Beg. It was Bir Beg and Verislov against Mahomet Khan—and the devil take the hindmost. It was a struggle to the death—a struggle to gain possession of the stolen guns. But in that event, where did the bales affair come in?

"Where is Mahomet Khan now?" he asked suddenly.

"We think, in Bombay."

Blake noted that "we". It confirmed his suspicions

that Verislov was speaking for himself and his new partner—Bir Beg.

"That's a lie!" he retorted promptly. "Mahomet Khan is here—here in Famipur!"

"Then you know more than I do, Sexton Blake. And more than any agent in the country knows—for we are all trying to find him."

The man was speaking truth, there, and Blake recognised it as such. He altered his tactics.

"When did he go to Bombay?" he asked.

"I don't know."

"Was it after the dacoity?"

"I don't know."

The detective smiled.

"Where did he hide what he took from those bales, Verislov?" he asked softly.

The smith's eyes lifted to Blake's face, clung for a moment, then as swiftly fell away. The brazier had died down to blackness by now, and the only illuminant was that flickering tallow dip, yet, dim as was the light, Blake had caught the unspoken question in the Russian's eyes—and was instantly on the trail.

"What did Mahomet Khan do with what he took from those bales, Verislov?" he asked again.

"I don't know."

"Did he leave it here?"

"No."

"Then what did he do with it?"

"I don't know."

With a sudden movement, Blake jammed his automatic hard against the other's ribs.

"Think again," he invited coldly.

"I've told you what he did with it—nothing!" the Russian answered stubbornly.

But Blake was hot on the trail now. The man had something to tell, and he must be made to tell it.

"Verislov," he warned, "I want the truth from you, and I'm determined to get it. Unless you want to have your interior arrangements spattered on the wall behind you, you'll realise that and tell me what I want to know. I'm asking you for the last time: what did Mahomet Khan do with what he took from those bales?"

The Russian's beady eyes swung this way and that across the room, but there was no escape.

"Fool!" he snarled, his eyes blazing with hate. "I've told you what he did. He didn't do anything!" But as Blake's finger whitened about the trigger of that gun: "He never had the chance to do anything!" he squealed.

"Why not?" Blake asked, in a dead level voice.

"He never had the stuff."

"Then who did?"

Crack!

A vicious streak of blue flame stabbed through the gloom of the alley outside, and in the same second the shop was plunged into darkness. Blake dived for Verislov's throat, but he was too late. So, too, was Tinker, who had launched himself bodily across the anvil in a flying tackle.

The thud of a bolt being shot home brought them to their feet, but by the time Blake had whipped out his torch the shop was empty. Paul Verislov had escaped through a door into the back regions.

"It's no use trying to break that in!" Blake snapped as his assistant threw himself against the inch-thick door. "Get round the back! Watch out for whoever fired that shot."

CHAPTER 12

BLAKE IS TRAPPED

THEY found a narrow passage running between the silversmith's house and the house next door, and at the top of that passage they encountered a ten-foot mud wall which appeared to enclose the whole of the silversmith's premises. There was no sign anywhere of the man who had fired that shot.

"One of Bir Beg's men?" Tinker whispered as they looked about them.

"Bir Beg would have shot at us—not the candle!" Blake said in a puzzled voice. "But it was Bir Beg who wrecked that train, and Bir Beg who looted the bales—I saw the name shaped on Verislov's lips when the candle was shot away!" He spoke sharply, as though chagrined that the explanation had not occurred to him before. "Over you go, Tinker!" he commanded a moment later. "There's no other way. Get through the house and open that other door for me—and shoot if you have to. Watch your step!"

He stooped, and Tinker mounted his shoulders. Blake straightened up, and with a heave and a jump Tinker got his hands to the top of the wall and swung himself astride. One glance was enough to show that the courtyard was empty. He dropped softly to the ground on the other side.

By the time Blake got back to that bolted door, Tinker had already opened it for him.

"He's gone, guv'nor!" he reported. "There isn't a soul in the place."

Blake followed him through, flashing his torch round the inner room as he went. Save for a charpoy and a few odds and ends it was empty. There was no exit from that room save through the door into the courtyard—and the courtyard, too, was empty.

"What about the well?" Blake asked, as he looked round.

The courtyard was perhaps twenty feet square. In the centre of it stood the household well.

The detectives approached that carefully, for its sides —of sun-baked brick—stood three feet or so above the level of the courtyard. It was equipped with a rough windlass from which dangled a chain. Blake peeped over the edge carefully, in case the Russian should be crouching just inside. And to make doubly sure, he shone his light vertically down the dangling chain.

"Guv'nor!" gasped Tinker suddenly. Blake steadied his torch. There was a wicked smile about the corners of his mouth—for he, too, had seen that cavity as quickly as Tinker, and as quickly guessed its import. There was a passage or tunnel of some kind hollowed out in the side of the well some fifteen to twenty feet down.

"That's where he's gone!" Tinker whispered.

"And that's where Bir Beg has hidden what he took from those bales!" Blake said tensely.

He switched off his torch, and listened. The night was very still. Not a sound was to be heard from anywhere, neither from the bazaar nor the well. Not even a pariah dog was barking.

Blake thought rapidly, re-arranging his facts in the light of what he now knew to be truth. Curiously enough, he had never once thought of that solution. He had never once thought that anyone else might have got in ahead of Mahomet Khan and looted the bales before he could get to them. Yet they had! And the man responsible was Bir Beg.

It was Bir Beg who had wrecked the train, and Bir Beg who had looted the bales. Bir Beg and Verislov between them. And they had done it as a set-off against Mahomet Khan's theft of the guns from the dump.

Mahomet Khan had consigned his bales to Peshawar, and in spite of what Christie had said about the Khyber Pass, it was evident that he had intended to take delivery of them there. But Verislov and Bir Beg had stymied his plan by wrecking the train outside Battock Station—and it was they, and not Mahomet Khan, who now possessed whatever it was that had been brought out in those bales.

Now Blake saw why Mahomet Khan had failed on the last lap. Now he understood why, in spite of all his carefully laid plans, Mahomet Khan had failed to win through across the border. Instead of Bir Beg running the guns affair, and Mahomet Khan the bales—as he told Winfield a few hours ago—it was Mahomet Khan who was running the guns, and Bir Beg the bales!

And in that event, instead of guns being put into that catafalque tomorrow, it would be whatever Bir Beg had taken from those ten bales of cotton-piece goods consigned by Tanner & Wild, of London, to Ram Dass, of Bombay.

It was the contents of the bales that was going into Bir Beg's catafalque!

"Watch the top here, Tinker!" Blake directed with sudden determination. "I'm going to have a look round that passage. Fire your revolver if there's trouble, and you want me. I'll be back in a quarter of an hour."

"Right-ho, guv'nor!" Tinker promised.

Slipping his torch into his pocket, and holding his automatic between his teeth, Blake threw a leg over the wall and seized the hanging chain. He curled it round his right leg, sailor-fashion, and slid easily into the depths below.

The darkness was Stygian, but he found the mouth of the passage and steadied himself opposite it. Then, freeing both hands and hanging by his legs alone, he took his torch in one hand and his revolver in the other, and switched on the light. He kept it on for a second only—just long enough to show him that the tunnel went deep into the earth, and was empty. Also he noticed a stout wooden bar fixed horizontally across the entrance.

He swung himself backwards and forwards across the well, kicking the back wall to give him momentum, and when the wooden bar came within his grasp, he grabbed it, pulled himself inwards, and landed quietly in the mouth of the tunnel.

Once under the bar and inside, he found it lower than he had thought. In places he had to drop to his hands and knees and crawl; but still the passage went on. Now and again he risked a flash from his torch to assure himself that no one was lying up for him and that the tunnel did not branch off anywhere—but the light revealed nothing save bare earth, and the tunnel went steadily onwards.

Then, after what he estimated to be some twelve yards

or so, the passage took an upward trend. Now Blake went very warily indeed, for he fancied that he must be nearing the outlet. Suddenly the walls fell away from beneath his hands, and in the same instant he became aware of muffled voices proceeding from somewhere in front of him.

He froze for a minute, listening. He tried to reach the wall on either side of him, but his groping fingers encountered nothing but space. He caught the impression that he was in a cellar of some kind, and that the voices were coming from above him—but in the pitch darkness it was difficult to be sure.

Yet he was sure of one thing—he was on the track of whatever had been taken from those bales! The only thing that surprised him was the size of the place. A hole in the wall—in the floor—would have been big enough to hold the contents of those ten bales. This place would accommodate an arsenal.

An arsenal! The phrase whipped his imagination to violent action. Was this where the original arms had been hidden? Was this the site of the arms dump the existence of which had shaken official India to its very core? Was this the place Mahomet Khan had robbed?

But then another thought struck him. If Mahomet Khan had robbed this place, quite obviously he would know of its existence. And in that event, surely, Bir Beg would never have hidden the contents of the bales here? He would have found some other hiding-place. Somewhere that Mahomet Khan did not know about, and could not find.

Those voices were silent now, and Blake crept forward again. Soon he came upon a chink of light ahead of him—a door! Yes, it was a door! And that door most probably led into the house of Bir Beg.

Inch by inch, feeling his way carefully across the uneven floor, Blake made his way towards that chink of light. Now it was almost within arm's reach of him. Another foot, and he was just about to apply his eye to the aperture when the distant roar of a gun boomed through the empty tunnel.

"Tinker!"

In a flash he saw what had happened. Now he understood why those voices ahead of him had so suddenly fallen to silence. Warned by Verislov of what had happened in his shop, the gang had raced round to the top of the well to make certain that their hiding-place had not been discovered. They were there now! That shot had been Tinker's! And even as the knowledge seared home to his understanding, someone began to unbolt the door in front of him.

Blake turned and fled. They had trapped him! There were men at the top of the well, and others following him down the tunnel. He wondered what had happened to Tinker? Wondered if the lad would manage to hold them at bay until he could climb the chain and come to his rescue?

Now he was near the mouth of the passage. Behind him he could hear stumbling footsteps following him at a great pace, but Blake was like a cat on his feet, and it might be that as yet they had not heard him in front of them. Warily he approached the spot where the tunnel opened sheer into the well.

Then he stopped. Voices! Voices—and lights!

The gang were in possession of the top of the well! He could hear them laughing and talking. High above the rest, Blake recognised the voice of the giant Afridi, Bir Beg—and he knew that the game was up. They had taken Tinker! The laughter he could hear was the soft, cruel laughter of men who find their enemy safely delivered into their hands.

The detective's eyes reddened. Above him was Bir Beg and his gang. Behind him were more of the gang. He could not get out up the well, nor could he get back along the tunnel. He was trapped.

Only one way remained open to him, and that—downwards!

To think, with Blake, was to act. He took that course with characteristic decision. A sudden gale of laughter above gave him the chance he needed, and he took it without hesitation. Leaning out in the darkness he found the chain and swung himself into space.

The chain ran through his hands noiselessly. In the pitch darkness he seemed to be sliding down miles. The air was thick and foetid—nauseating—and almost unbreathably foul. He thought of all he had ever heard about the loathsome snakes that made their nests in the wells of India. He pictured them squirming and sliding over each other down there in the depths—waiting for him. But still he went down. The water was his only chance and he had to take it.

Finally, just when he was beginning to think the well bottomless, his feet touched water. He lowered himself into it up to his neck, restraining his gasping breaths and ignoring the foul odour which threatened to gas him. Then he looked up.

It was like looking through the wrong end of a telescope. Far away above him was a tiny circle of star-spangled sky—so ineffably remote as to appear quite unreal. So distant that he wondered if he would ever be able to climb up to it again. And as he watched, a thread-like arm reached out of the tunnel to seize the chain.

Blake released it instantly and floated free. Even in that heady crisis his wits did not desert him. If anyone were to reach out for that chain and feel it taut beneath his hands he would know in a moment that it had a weight attached somewhere—and that could mean only one thing. It would mean that Blake himself had gone down the well instead of back into the passage or up to the surface.

The chain rocked in the water as the man up above swung out from the tunnel and climbed steadily to the well-head. He was going to make his report. The moment Blake saw his bulk disappear from against the stars, he knew he had reached the top and stepped out into the courtyard. Then he caught hold of the chain for a moment and rested.

He wondered what Bir Beg would do now. Would he pull up the chain and so "seal" his tunnel for the night? Blake closed his eyes at the thought; closed his eyes and turned sick with horror as he envisaged himself being left to drown like a rat in those noisome depths—but he thrust the thought from him. Like all brave men, he refused to meet death before it came. Anxiously he watched that circle of stars, apprehensive, but ready for all emergencies.

It came sooner than he had bargained for. Someone thrust a lighted torch over the side and peered down. Blake knew that the light could not penetrate to where he was lying awash in the ice-cold water, but nevertheless he sank deeper into the slime. It was well that he did, for the next moment the torch was released and came hissing down the well shaft like a blazing comet, bumping from side to side.

Blake forced himself deeper. Farther down the water was colder still, and he stayed down until his lungs were bursting—then broke water again.

The light was gone. The remnants of the torch were there beside him on the surface, cold, and dead.

And thank God!—the chain was still there!

How long he waited Blake never knew. He intended to give the men ten minutes before he started to climb back to the top, but whether he gave them ten days or ten centuries he did not know. Waiting in the darkness, among the slime and the filth, it might easily have been ten aeons.

When at last he did start to climb, his fingers were almost too numb to grasp the chain. As he hauled himself free of the water, the drip from his clothes sounded as loud as the Niagara Falls—but nothing happened. No black obscured the sweet stars above, and no one challenged him.

He climbed on.

CHAPTER 13

THE BODY IN THE DARK

WHEN eventually Blake found himself opposite the mouth of the gallery, he did not hesitate. Throughout the whole of that muscle-breaking climb his brain had been working at top speed, and he knew precisely what he was going to do. Instinct told him that even if Bir Beg had killed Tinker, he would not risk leaving the body in the open courtyard. Nor would he leave it in the silversmith's shop—in view of what Verislov himself feared from Blake. He would take it to his own house and hide it in the tunnel. And if he had merely taken Tinker prisoner, the same line of reasoning held good. He would take him to his own house and there keep him secure.

Therefore, when Blake reached the level of the tunnel, he began to swing himself to and fro across the well. Presently he was able to seize the wooden bar and haul himself inwards. A minute later he was lying flat on his back on the floor of the passage, recovering his breath and relaxing his muscles.

Then, when he was sufficiently rested, he fetched out his automatic and carefully took out the magazine. Cartridge by cartridge he wiped them dry in his hands, wrung out a corner of his Madrassi's robe, and then wiped dry the chamber—afterwards waving everything to and fro in the hot air of the tunnel to complete the treatment. He knew he could not rely absolutely upon the cartridges, but he remembered occasions before when he had had to swim for it and afterwards found the cartridges fireable. In any case, he could but hope for the best.

Satisfied that he had done everything humanly possible, he turned and began the slow crawl back to where he had seen that chink of light at the end of the tunnel. This time it did not seem so far, and soon he became aware of a

single voice speaking. He listened to it as he crept forward
—and wondered. There was only one voice—no one was
answering—and as he drew nearer Blake was struck by a
peculiar quality in that voice. It was a taunting voice.
It sounded as though someone were taunting a helpless
man—a man who could not answer back. And suddenly
Blake's blood ran cold.

Were they subjecting Tinker to torture?

The thought galvanised him to action. In the darkness
his eyes narrowed dangerously. He tried his torch with
the bulb pressed close to the floor, but it was useless.

The chink of light was quite close now, and the voice
clearer. It sounded to Blake like the voice of Bir Beg—but
he could not be sure. Nor could he recognise what
language the man was using.

He crawled on another foot or two, and then something
occurred which momentarily shattered even Sexton
Blake's iron nerves. He was on his hands and knees when
suddenly his right hand came down on something cold
and soft. For a second he remained motionless, frozen.
His first thought was that he had touched a snake, but
almost immediately he realised his error. The thing under
his hand was a man's face.

"Tinker!" his lips formed soundlessly.

With a herculean effort, Blake steadied himself. If
only it were not so dark! Holding his breath, he moved
his hand lightly over the dead face. Then he breathed again.

It was not Tinker. This man had a clean-shaven face,
but his hair was long, and matted, and coarse. Reassured
on that point, with a steadier hand Blake went over him
again. There was a thin chain round the man's neck,
stubbed here and there with beads—a fakir's rosary.
That long, matted hair was the hair of a fakir. Blake felt
the stuff of his robe—it was rough and dirty. The holy man!

It came to Blake in a flash. The holy man! The man
for whose body those Wardakis cut-throats were coming
in the morning. He had been carried into the tunnel and
left there—thrown there, like a dog. Blake recalled the

words of Winfield's corporal: "Does Bir Beg—dacoit, thief, gun-runner, cut-throat!—does Bir Beg care two straws for any holy man living? Then why should he care for one dead?"

Blake smiled to himself grimly. The corporal had been right. Bir Beg did not care. That holy man was merely an excuse. He had served his purpose, and Bir Beg had flung him out into the tunnel to rot. It was not a holy man, but the contents of those ten bales that was going into the catafalque tomorrow! Not guns, as Winfield thought, but the contents of those ten bales of cotton-piece goods shipped by Tanner & Wild, of London, to Ram Dass, of Bombay.

They had travelled far since that night when little Mr. Tanner had first mentioned them to Blake in his Baker Street home, but he was up with them now! The stuff was there under his hand, somewhere, and he would find it, if he had to tear down the place lath by lath!

Now he was at the door, and, raising himself cautiously, he applied his eye to the chink. To his disappointment he could see nothing, but he soon realised that that was because someone was standing directly in front of him upon the other side.

But it was Bir Beg speaking, and his voice was ugly. He was speaking in Persian, but Blake could not catch the meaning, although he was asking the same question over and over again. But there was no answer.

Then whoever was standing in Blake's way, moved. Simultaneously there was a dull thud and an exclamation, as though someone had been struck. Then Blake saw, and the breath caught hot in his throat.

Lying there, bound and helpless, on a charpoy, with half his beard torn off, and with blood streaming down his face, was none other than Ali Singh.

Ali Singh!

.   .   .   .   .

Blake stood for a moment dumb-founded. How in the world did Ali Singh come to be there, and in that shape?

Even as he stared at the man, Bir Beg put that same question again, and when Ali Singh laughed his derision, the Afridi struck him once more, full across his mouth.

A thin trickle of blood bore mute witness to the agent's agony.

Blake saw red. Insinuating his fingers into the crack of the door, he was surprised to find that it moved. Bir Beg must have opened it to throw out the body of the holy man, and either forgotten, or not bothered, to bolt it again.

Now Bir Beg had a knife in his hand. It was across Ali Singh's throat, and again Blake heard that same question.

Blake eased the door another inch or two. Now he could see into the room, which appeared to be an underground cellar of some kind. It was lit by a tallow dip stuck on the wall, and a rough ladder led up to a closed trapdoor in the roof. Blake eyed that ladder carefully. Bir Beg and Ali Singh were alone in the cellar, but the gang were within easy call up above.

All that, Blake saw at a glance. Then he saw that Bir Beg was putting slow pressure on that knife. There was blood beneath its cutting edge, and Ali Singh's eyes were dark with agony, but even in extremis he would not speak. Game to the last was Ali Singh.

Blake clubbed his revolver. He dare not risk a shot, nor dare he give Bir Beg a chance to call for help. He steadied himself. In one single movement he thrust back the door and leapt.

Crack! He brought down the butt of his revolver cleanly on the back of Bir Beg's head. The fellow's turban was thick, but Blake's wrists were of steel, and he had struck scientifically. The gun-runner crumpled where he stood, and Blake—to save the noise of his fall—caught him in his arms and lowered him gently to the ground.

Ali Singh, who had stared at him open-mouthed for a moment, was the first to recover his tongue.

"As old hymn says, sahib," he whispered, "one swallow

too many spoil the broth. I think so. Like early bird, sahib, you arrive in crack of time as we say."

"Where's Tinker?" Blake snapped as he cut the man free.

"Gone for assistance, sahib. Bir Beg's faithless ones surprised us at the well, and Tinker sahib ran for assistance, but me they caught. Bir Beg tore at my beard, and when half of it came away in his hand, he gave roar like big bull of Bashan, as we say. He remember me from when I am here before, working on that arms scare. 'Spy of the Sirkar!' he shout. And all his men shout with him. Then band begin to play, as we say."

Blake heaved a sigh of relief. Tinker was safe! His eyes swept to that closed trapdoor.

"Come on!" he whispered. "We'd better get out of here!"

He turned and led the way back along the tunnel. If Tinker had gone for assistance, he would be back any time now. It would be a simple matter to post a few men at the top of the well and take round the remainder to Bir Beg's house. Then, forcing the door, they would compel the rats to escape down the tunnel and catch them one by one as they climbed out of the well.

After that, he himself would search the place for the contents of those ten bales.

.   .   .   .   .

Blake was first to reach the cooler air of the courtyard, and he waited impatiently for Ali Singh to follow him. When, a few minutes later, the agent did appear, he apologised for keeping the sahib waiting.

"I remembered that that faithless one had taken my Gold Eagle," he said, "so I went back for it."

"You should have left it there, man!" Blake told him, but Ali Singh shook his head.

"It is a matter concerning my izzat, sahib," he said, with a dignity that quite startled the detective. You would have thought him a king by the way he pronounced that word "izzat". "It is a matter concerning my izzat, sahib," he said. "My honour."

"Oh, all right!" Blake shrugged the detail aside. "How did you come to be at the top of this well," he asked, "when I left you safely in the bungalow?"

The native smiled—a painful process by the look of things. Usually, that smile of his was naive and childlike—curiously disarming—but now, in the moonlight, with his face smeared with blood, and with only half a tousled beard decorating his chin, he looked positively sinister!

"My orders from Major Christie sahib were to watch you same like dog," he answered. "Therefore, when I saw the sahibs leaving bungalow, I briskly girded up loins, as we say, and followed in warm pursuit."

Blake understood. Perhaps it was just as well that he had followed them, the way things had fallen out.

"And now listen," he said. "Things are moving, Ali Singh! I've discovered tonight that it was not Mahomet Khan who wrecked that train, but Bir Beg!"

The agent showed no surprise.

"I learn that same thing, huzoor," he said instantly. "That faithless one taunted me with the information, back there in that cellar."

"Did he say what it was he stole?"

The agent shook his head.

"But he say one thing, sahib, that——"

"That what?" Blake pounced.

The man hesitated. He appeared rather uncertain.

"Only Allah himself can judge between truth and lies when spoken by that faithless one," he apologised then. "But he say to me, sahib—he tell me that Mahomet Khan has already stolen the guns from that arms dump, and——"

"That's true, anyhow!" Blake cut in. "That's something else I heard tonight. And that, incidentally, is why Bir Beg wrecked and looted those bales."

"Even so, sahib. But I hear more than that. I hear

that all the guns from that arms dump are now safe across border!"

"What?"

"Safe across border, sahib!" the man repeated. "Mahomet Khan not only rifle that dump, but he run every single gun from there safely across border to his own place! Now nothing left!"

Blake stood rigid. For a moment he stared at the agent incredulously. All those guns over the border! It was impossible! It was incredible! And yet——

He thought swiftly. Verislov had admitted that he did now know where the guns were. Supposing Ali Singh were right? Supposing Mahomet Khan had run the things safely across the border? Was it possible that Verislov was holding on to what he had taken from those bales in order to use it as lever to make Mahomet Khan return what he had stolen? Was that the scheme? But if Mahomet Khan had his guns safe across the border, why should he risk his neck with this bale business at all? Unless, of course, the bales were in some way complimentary to the arms.

"Was this where they were stolen from?" he asked Ali Singh suddenly.

"Nay, sahib. The first dump was near Peshawar, and that is where the guns were taken from. Bir Beg and that faithless one, Abdul Aza, make this place. Make it secretly."

"What—for the handful of stuff they took from those bales?" Blake asked incredulously.

The agent shook his head.

"This place is old," he pointed out. "If sahib noticed, earth already very dry. No," he said. "In opinion of self, sahib, Bir Beg and Abdul Aza planned to remove guns from first hiding-place and hide again here."

"Why?"

"Can only suggest, sahib, that Bir Beg insist upon same. Guns no good to Bir Beg while in Peshawar. Bir Beg belong here, sahib. His home is just across the border, and all his friends. 'Bring guns here,' he would say to Abdul Aza, 'and I buy.' I think so."

"Yes." Blake spoke slowly. Now he was beginning to see daylight. Now things were beginning to fall into place.

Verislov had supplied those arms to the order of Mahomet Khan—the first Mahomet Khan, the one Government had hanged. And they had hanged him before he could take delivery—maybe before he had paid for the stuff. That had left Verislov in an awkward position, since he could neither get the guns backwards nor forwards. He had thereupon done the only thing possible—sat down and waited. And when the hue and cry died down, he had got into touch with the next biggest man along the border—Bir Beg.

He had offered the guns to Bir Beg, and Bir Beg had agreed to buy subject to the guns being delivered in Famipur—in his own territory. Verislov had then moved to Famipur, and between them they had excavated the tunnel and made everything ready for the reception of the consignment.

But upon going back to arrange for the removal, Verislov had found that other dump empty! Mahomet Khan—this new Mahomet Khan—had got in first, and completely cleared the place!

Later, Mahomet Khan must have gone to England to arrange the bales business, but there he had not been so fortunate. Either Verislov or Bir Beg had got wind of the trip and set their spies to await Mahomet Khan's return to India. It occurred to Blake, in parenthesis, that Mahomet Khan had recognised that labourer at the gate of the docks as a spy, and duly strangled him. But that apart, Bir Beg had known of the bales, and wrecked the train outside Battock station, thus getting, at any rate, some hold over the man who had duped him. Whatever had been in those bales was now in the hands of Bir Beg and Verislov.

And that was what was going into the catafalque tomorrow!

Blake smiled to himself. Things were moving now.

"Mahomet Khan doesn't know of this tunnel, of course?" he said to the agent.

"Nay, sahib. That his trouble. I think he know Bir Beg and Abdul Aza steal his bales, but he not know where they hide the loot. But he no fool, sahib, that Mahomet Khan!"

"You're right there!" Blake agreed shortly. "But go on!"

"He no fool, sahib," the agent continued. "As soon as he hear of the funeral party and the catafalque, he smell big rat, as we say. He may not know where loot is hidden, but he will know where to look for it when that funeral party starts back to border, and that is what Bir Beg fears. That is why he keep asking me in that cellar. 'Where is Mahomet Khan? Where is Mahomet Khan? Where is Mahomet Khan?' "

"So that's what he was asking—eh?" Blake smiled.

"Because he afraid, sahib. He fear that Mahomet Khan will lie up for him on road to pass. He fear that Mahomet Khan will attack catafalque, and even at nineteenth hour, as we say, win back what those faithless ones took from those bales. I think so."

"And so do I!" Blake smiled thinly and rubbed his hands. Here was the chance he had been waiting for. If they could set a trap, so could he! Instead of arresting Bir Beg tonight, he would leave him. He would leave him free to carry out his plans. He should pack his stolen loot in that catafalque, and trail it up the road to the pass as bait for Mahomet Khan. And when Mahomet Khan leapt, Blake would leap, too!

"Look here, Ali Singh!" he said suddenly. "You cut along after Tinker sahib and turn those police back. Tell Tinker sahib all that has happened, and tell him to go back and wait for me in the bungalow. We'll let Bir Beg get on with his procession. We'll let him take that loot, and then we'll sit back and watch what happens. We can always stop him at the pass, in any event. Tell Tinker sahib that I'm going to wait in the room he knows of until the procession leaves here in the morning. Then I'll come along to the bungalow. Understand?"

The agent looked at him a bit doubtfully.

"Is that—wise, sahib?" he asked at last.

"It's going to be done, anyway!" Blake laughed. "Now off you go, and at all costs keep those police from interfering in the bazaar until morning."

The agent gave in with a shrug.

"It is as the sahib wills," he said formally. "We are all in the hands of Allah—the Merciful, the Compassionate?" He turned silently on his heel and faded like a shadow into the darkness.

Alone, Blake turned his attention to the windlass. Reaching out, he unhooked the chain from its staple and allowed it to fall crashing into the water. It fell with enough noise to waken the dead, apparently, but nothing happened. In the bazaars of India, after dark, every man concerns himself only with his own affairs. Then, secure in the knowledge that he had sealed one end of the secret tunnel, he followed Ali Singh into the street.

Not a sound broke the silence of the hot night. Not a thing was stirring anywhere. Feeling his way along the rough mud wall, stumbling over the garbage heaps, he at last found his way to the room Winfield had hired for Tinker's spying activities.

The door opened to his touch. He went inside. The place was like an oven, the blackness Stygian. He closed the door behind him, and was just feeling for his torch when something descended with crushing force upon his head.

His world split into a million searing fragments. A white hot pain shot down his spine. He felt himself falling; felt hot hands groping at his throat. Then oblivion.

CHAPTER 14

THE CONTENTS OF THE CATAFALQUE

It was still dark when Captain James Winfield rose from his bed the next morning. The stars were wavering like guttering candles in the chill wind that blows up the dawn. The moon was gone. The flat expanse of the plain rolled away dimly to the distant mountains, but below Abbabi Pass—where last night he had seen the watch-fires of the funeral party—all was now a uniform darkness.

He dressed quickly and went off to say good morning to his guests. Neither was there, nor had their beds been slept in. That surprised him; worried him, too. He stood for a moment frowning, then went out to find Ali Singh. But Ali Singh, too, was missing, and his own bearer told him that the sahibs' bearer had been out all night, and was not yet returned.

"He followed his sahibs, huzoor," the man said.

So they were all out! Winfield thought for a moment, and then went back into his bungalow. He supposed they were all right! Blake had warned him never to worry if he did not turn up when expected. Likely enough he had found Mahomet Khan, and was lying in wait for him—maybe miles away. In any event there was nothing he could do about it, and meanwhile he had his own work to consider.

He went down to the horse-lines. He found the havildar already gone, and the corporal on the point of leaving. He assured himself that the man understood his instructions, and then passed along to "stables". It was nearly six o'clock by the time he got back to the bungalow, and still there was no sign of the missing men.

At half-past six his orderly came in with information that the funeral party had been observed coming down the road. Winfield ate his breakfast, waited another hour, and then—warned by a cacophonous braying of horns and clashing of cymbals that they were somewhere near —he slipped his revolver into its holster, crossed his compound, and went down to the white road to wait.

The procession was coming along slowly. In the van, borne high upon the shoulders of four men, was the saffron-coloured palanquin containing the inevitable "holy man" without which no funeral procession is reckoned complete. Behind that, carried by four other men, was a wooden catafalque of such dimensions as caused Winfield to smile. The thing was enormous— bigger even that his corporal had suggested. It would have held half a dozen men—easily; and was out of all proportion to the holiness of the body it was destined to receive. To Winfield's heated imagination it seemed simply to shriek aloud its real purpose. Behind that again straggled the spare carriers, and it was they who were responsible for the heartening music.

As they came nearer, Winfield took careful stock of the men themselves. The nearer they came, the less he liked them. They were all Wardakis—ragged, hook-nosed, high-cheekboned devils who would slit a man's throat as soon as look at him, and revel in the chance. Fierce-eyed, heavily-bearded ruffians, shouting and singing and being rapidly whipped to a species of frenzy by the horns and cymbals of their brothers. He was positively certain that beneath their rags every man-jack of them was armed to the teeth, and he cursed the fool politicals who had not thought to put a clause concerning arms in the safe-conduct.

"Halt them when they get opposite," he said to his havildar, "and bring me their safe-conduct. Make it snappy!"

The sergeant saluted and stepped into the middle of the road. At sight of him the bearers set down the wooden catafalque with surprising obedience, but the saffron-coloured palanquin continued impudently on its way.

"Halt, there!" roared the havildar furiously.

A stream of appalling language issued from inside the thing, and almost immediately it, too, was lowered to the ground.

"Get the safe-conduct!" Winfield ordered sharply. But before the sergeant could move, the curtains were pulled back from the inside, and it became evident that the holy man in charge was about to descend. The four carriers, freed of their burden, started to push and pull at him as though dragging a bullock from its stall; and presently, with a gasp and a groan, out popped the fattest little man Winfield had ever seen. He was dressed in the usual saffron robe, huge, horn-rimmed spectacles.

They set him on his feet, and he waddled towards Winfield like some outlandish duck. He was completely bald and round as a barrel.

Winfield stared at him in amazement.

"Pardon these asses of mine, captain," he called in Pushtu, as he came within speaking range. "They did but try to save the legs of Holiness."

"Who are you?" Winfield asked shortly.

"The priest in charge, captain."

"Show me your safe-conduct!"

Obediently the fakir fumbled beneath his robe and presently brought to light the required document. Winfield scanned it carefully.

"Do we pass, captain?" the fat one asked at last.

"You do!" Winfield was curt. He handed him back the paper and waved him to proceed. "And watch that you're back over the border by sunset!" he called after him.

"We have beds there, captain," the fakir replied cryptically.

He squeezed back into the palanquin, and the bearers hoisted it on to their shoulders with a shout. Up went the big catafalque, and that, too, went by with a shout. But as Winfield studied its proportions his resolution increased; and when one of its carriers laughed at him impudently, he knew that sacrilege or no sacrilege, he was going to examine the inside of it before it was carried back over the border that night. But first of all he would ring up the politicals across the border for the necessary authority. He glanced at his watch. It was a quarter to eight. They would not be there until nine so that he had an hour and a quarter to wait.

He turned to his havildar.

"Well, what did you think of them?" he asked.

The man shook his head. He seemed undecided.

"That fat fakir, sahib," he said at last, "was once the friend of Mahomet Khan—him whom the sirkar hanged. He was with him in that affair at Ghazni Kul, when they fell upon our outpost there—in Major Charles sahib's time, it was! The sirkar put a price on his head for that, sahib."

"Mahomet Khan's man, eh?" Winfield mused. "Now helping Mahomet Khan's successor, Bir Beg?" He gave a short laugh. "The king is dead—long live the king, havildar—what?"

The havildar did not reply. The allusion was over his head. He watched the departing procession in silence for a moment, then:

"I wonder why he got out of that palanquin, sahib?" he said thoughtfully.

Winfield looked at the man.

"Why shouldn't he?" he asked.

"Well, there is still a price on his head, sahib."

"Maybe! But he's safe enough today, havildar, in any event. He's here under Government safe-conduct, remember!"

He dismissed the havildar with a gesture and walked on up to his bungalow.

"Hallo?" he exclaimed as Judy Kershaw rose from a low chair to greet him. "I thought I asked you to stay in your bungalow today?"

"So you did, but I thought I'd stay in yours!" she laughed at him cheerfully. "Well, how did it go?"

He told her, repeating what the havildar had just told him about the fat fakir. He also told her that Blake, Tinker, and Ali Singh, had not returned from their mysterious mission into the bazaar.

"I don't like that," she said at once. "That's bad."

"Why? What do you think has happened to them?"

She answered him with another question.

"Why do you think that fakir came out of his palanquin?"

"Sheer impudence!" Winfield said. "Bravado! He knows nobody can touch him while he is travelling under Government safe-conduct."

"That all?" she smiled.

"Well, why do you think he came out?"

"To show himself," she said quietly.

.   .   .   .   .

There was a long silence. Winfield stood staring out of the window, his eyes wrinkled in thought. Finally he reached for a cigarette.

"What exactly do you mean by that?" he asked at last, with obvious reluctance.

"What I say," the girl answered. "There is something fishy about this procession business, Jimmy. I thought so last night—so did Mr. Blake. In fact, that's why he went down to the bazaar last night—and you see the result? None of them is back yet."

"I don't think you need worry yourself about Sexton Blake," Winfield assured her easily. "Besides, that is side-tracking the issue. You were speaking of the procession—why do you say it's fishy?"

She ignored his heavy sarcasm.

"Those people want you to think they're gun-running," she said in her level tones, "and you do think it. They primed your corporal, last night. They allowed him to hear what they wanted him to hear, and see what they intended him to see—well knowing that he would run to you with his story. They bring a perfectly monstrous catafalque which simply shrieks to be looked into! That fat fakir—a famous dacoit with a price on his head——steps cheerfully from his palanquin and says: 'Look at me, sahib! You know me! What do you think I'm here for, eh? Think a man like me has come all this way for a miserable holy man? Not likely!"

"Is this an exhibition of second sight?" Winfield interrupted in his coolest manner.

"Oh, don't be silly! It just happens that I was born and brought up out here, Jimmy, and I know these people. I can read them like a book, and that's why I can see 'bait' written in huge letters all over that catafalque. This procession has been deliberately planned with one end in view. And that—to make you look into their catafalque! The smiles of the carriers; the foolishness of that fakir in showing himself—when he need not have done! Everything points to a trap."

"But in God's name—why?" Winfield burst out irritably. "You keep on talking about 'bait' and 'traps', but what's the object of it all? What do they want?"

"Well, first of all, they want those arms, I suppose——"

"Oh, you do agree that they're gun-running, then?"

"Yes, but not in the way you think. This procession is just a trap, and the bait is that large-sized catafalque."

"Well, what do you suggest I do about it all?"

"Nothing," she said. "Sit back and do nothing. Block their plans by refusing to take their bait——"

"And let them walk those rifles out of the country without let or hindrance?" he laughed loudly. "I should say so! By gosh, I should say so!" He looked at the clock on the shelf and rose swiftly to his feet. "No, my child!" he said. "I'm a policeman, and my duty is to scotch little jobs of this kind before ever they get a chance to get properly going. Those blighters think they've got me guessing, but they're wrong! I'm going to ring through now to the political agent telling him what I think about everything and just what I intend to do. I shan't be long."

He stalked into his office, pressed down the switch, and turned the handbell of his telephone. He turned it again. He waited for a minute or two, and tried it yet a third time.

Suddenly his eyes narrowed, and he picked up the receiver. There was no familiar hum. With the receiver still pressed to his ear he turned the handbell.

"Can't you get him?" Judy's voice came from the next room.

"No; they've cut the wire!" His voice was faintly triumphant. He stalked into the other room. "The line's dead as mutton!" he announced. "That shows you, doesn't it? Last night they cut the wire between me and police headquarters. This morning they've cut it between me and the political department. They think I'll be afraid to act without the necessary authority, but that's where they're wrong, as I told Blake last night." He turned to his orderly: "Tell Havildar Bussul Khan to attend me here instantly!" he rapped out. And without a glance at Judy he went back to his office.

He sat down at his desk and began to write rapidly. It was a brief resume of the morning's happenings, addressed to headquarters and marked "By Hand". A rider would have to cross the fifty miles of desert with it, but even so it would reach headquarters before nightfall.

By the time he had finished it was close on ten o'clock, and at eleven, having given full instructions to his havildar, he mounted his horse and rode off in the direction of Abbabi Pass. Everything was now clear in his mind. He knew exactly what he was going to do, and precisely where he was going to do it. That cut telephone wire had settled the business once and for all. They had shown their hand, and Captain James Winfield was not the man to ask for a second look. One was quite sufficient for him.

Midday found him patiently awaiting the returning procession in a deep defile some eight miles from his bungalow. He had hobbled his horse in a nearby nullah, and had chosen the defile because of the privacy it

E

afforded. He was fully aware of the dangerousness of what he was about to attempt, but if the rifles were there the sacrilege would be justified. If they were not, no one would have seen him save those in the actual procession—and for that mob of cutthroats he did not care.

He waited a long time. The heat was by now terrific. The sun was almost directly overhead, and he was assailed by a veritable army of flies. His whisk was never still. Not a tree was in sight. Not a single square inch of shade. The sun hung like a molten ball in a sky that was of yellow brass.

It was close on three o'clock before he heard the sounds for which he was waiting.

He got up, then, and loosened his revolver in its holster. His plan was simplicity itself. He proposed to halt the procession under pretext of examining their safe-conduct again, get that fat fakir out of his palanquin, jam his revolver into the fellow's ribs, and demand to be shown what was in the catafalque. If the rifles were there, he would order the carriers to march straight back to Famipur under threat of shooting their leader. If they were not there—well, he would withdraw as gracefully as possible. But they were there! Of that he was absolutely convinced.

Presently the funeral party came over the brow of the dip, and the leaders saw Winfield standing at his ease in the middle of the road, obviously barring their passage. He held up his hand, and after a scarcely perceptible hesitation the four sweating bearers slid to a halt. If they were surprised to see him they gave no sign. Hard behind the palanquin came the catafalque—and that, too, was halted and set down in the white dust.

Then Winfield made his first mistake. Instead of standing where he was and calling the fakir to come to him, he walked purposefully to the palanquin and jerked aside the saffron curtains. Perhaps he was over-anxious to get the fat fakir at the end of his revolver. Perhaps he misjudged the mettle of the men he was dealing with. In any event, even as his fingers touched the curtain, he was aware of the fact that the men had closed in on him, effectually cutting off his retreat.

But he did not show that he had noticed the movement.

"Come out!" he ordered the fakir peremptorily. "I wish to speak with you."

"What does the sahib desire?" the man asked, obediently squeezing himself through the narrow doorway.

Winfield looked at him. He did not like the man. He was too suave, too smiling. He had a trump card up his sleeve, but it was too late to draw back now. With great deliberation he said:

"I intend to look in that catafalque of yours."

The fakir's expression did not alter. For all the dismay or surprise he showed the request might have been a perfectly usual one.

"The sahib is doubtless aware of the consequence of such a demand?" was all he said.

"I'm risking that!"

One of the men behind him began to mutter maledictions, but Winfield stood his ground. The fakir shrugged his fat shoulders.

"What is to be, will be!" he said, with pious resignation. "Come with me, sahib, if you are determined upon this evil course."

Winfield wavered. Such readiness on the fakir's part argued innocence—unless it was bluff. But it was bluff. It was bluff. He remembered what the corporal had told him of their conversation last night. He remembered the cut wires, the whole conduct of the affair. They were trying by an assumption of resigned willingness to bluff him out of doing what he had come to do.

Stiffening his resolution, Winfield followed the fakir to the catafalque.

"Open!" the fakir said to his men.

Muttering and cursing below their breath, the men lifted the big lid. Instantly Winfield smelt death—but that was nothing. He quite expected the dead holy man to be lying on top of the guns.

The fakir drew back.

"Look!" he invited softly.

Instead, Winfield looked at the circle of fierce faces ranged about him. He read their thoughts easily. They were waiting for him to turn his back, but he had no intention of obliging them. Snatching out his revolver he clamped it hard against the fakir's fat side.

"If any one of you as much as moves his little finger— the fakir dies!" he rasped. Then he turned to the catafalque.

He was disappointed. He could see nothing—nothing save the outline of a body hidden beneath a dirty cloth.

"Take that cloth away!" he ordered the fakir.

"The sight will not be pleasant to the sahib's eyes," the fakir warned.

"Take it away, I said!"

The fakir shrugged. He leaned over the side of the catafalque and lifted the cloth clear.

"Take your fill, O foolish one!" he jibed.

Winfield leaned over, braced for anything; but, even as he looked down, the breath caught sharply in his throat. He gave a funny little gasping sound. Was he mad, or dreaming? Or crazy—or what?

There were two bodies there! The first he recognised as that of Abdul Aza, the silversmith—with its throat cut. The second—that face half-hidden by bandages—that mouth stopped with a cruel gag—those beseeching eyes. His heart gave a sickening lurch.

The next second he spun round with an oath—too late. He had a fleeting impression of fierce eyes and flashing teeth, and the next instant received a stunning blow on his head. There was a jagged sheet of flame, a dull roar, and even as the thought flashed across his mind that Judy had been right, after all, he lost consciousness.

CHAPTER 15

THE END OF BIR BEG

SEXTON Blake awoke to find that it was still night. For a time he lay motionless, trying in vain to orientate himself. The blackness was thick and oppressive—almost tangible. His head ached violently. Every muscle in his body felt sore and strained, but when he tried to alter his position he found himself held fast by giant hands.

But Blake had a wonderful physique, and soon his mind rose triumphant over his physical limitations. He realised that he was bound hand and foot, trussed like a fowl. He was on the ground, for when he moved his fingers he could feel earth beneath his scratching nails.

Then he remembered. The well—that room—that sickening crack on his head. He remembered those thin fingers feeling for his throat in the blackness. Tinker! Ali Singh!

He closed his eyes for a moment as a sudden wave of nausea shook him from head to heel. He was sick and hungry. He must have lain there for hours—lain there in the same position, cramped and twisted. Yet it was still dark. It was still night. Unless there were shutters over the window.

He worked himself round on the bare floor, but in every direction he was met with the same blank darkness. He tore frantically at the bonds confining his wrists, but they were immovable. Whoever had trussed him up was no amateur at the game. It would take him hours to free himself of those ropes.

Puzzled by the intense blackness, Blake lay still again. Not a sound reached his straining ears. The silence was so heavy that it seemed almost to scream at him—yet the bazaar could never be as silent as that.

He worked himself sideways, tried to roll over, but

failed. The floor seemed to go up in a curve. He tried the
other way, but found himself faced with the same dilem-
ma. He was lying in a channel of some kind. A narrow
passage. A tunnel.

"A tunnel!" he thought swiftly. That was it. That
would explain the darkness, the dead silence. They had
taken him from that room opposite the silversmith's shop
and hidden him in the tunnel. It might be any time. It
might be morning, afternoon, or even evening. The
procession might have gone away hours ago. Mahomet
Khan and his loot might by this time be miles over the
border in the safety of his own country.

The thought drove Blake to frenzy, but he did not make
the mistake of tearing like a madman at his bonds. Not
that way would he free himself. It would take time—
time, and all the patience he could muster.

He set about the job scientifically. First he bent himself
double in an attempt to get his teeth to the rope about his
legs, but they were tied below his knees, and he could not
reach them. His ankles were similarly bound. If only he
could get his hands free—but his wrists were bound
behind him, and he had no knife upon which he could
lie. He tried rubbing his wrists against the earth with the
idea of fraying the rope, but the earth was too soft to
make an impression.

His only chance, he realised, lay in alternatively ex-
panding and contracting his muscles until he could slip a
hand through the stretched and loosened rope.

Much has been said of Sexton Blake's strength of wrist.
His untiring patience, his unflagging perseverance, have
long since become a legend among those who know him
best. But Blake himself is the first to admit that never
before or since has he struggled as he struggled then in
that tunnel. At times he was almost in despair. After
what seemed years of steady, concentrated labour those
ropes seemed taut as ever. He thought they never would
loosen. But perseverance told. Not even those stout ropes
could hold for ever against the swell and fall of the

detective's straining muscles, and suddenly—most miraculously as it seemed to Blake—one of his hands came free.

After that, of course, it was comparatively easy. In a very few minutes he had untied his legs and feet and was able to stand upright. Within ten minutes of freeing that first hand Sexton Blake was on his feet once more—stiff and sore, it is true—but otherwise ready for anything.

And his first job was to get out of that tunnel.

Scouting forward, he presently found himself approaching daylight. That would be where the tunnel opened out into the side of the well. Unfortunately, Blake remembered, there was no exit that way now—since he himself had thrown the chain into the water only last night. A mistake that, he realised, as he approached the end.

Holding on to the wooden bar which crossed from side to side of the mouth of the tunnel, Blake looked up the well. From the bright sunlight that came streaming down, almost blinding him in its intensity, he realised to his dismay that it must be close on high noon. In that case the procession would have already started, so that he had no time to lose.

He scrambled back along the tunnel. The only exit now lay through Bir Beg's house, and what he would encounter in that direction he scarcely dared to think. He felt for his revolver, but found it gone. His torch, too, was gone. He had nothing save his bare fists—but he was not dismayed. Few men could give a better account of themselves in a rough house than Sexton Blake.

Soon the sides of the passage opened out, and he knew himself to be back in the cellar beneath Bir Beg's house. Groping forward carefully, warned by his nose that the dead holy man was still there, Blake reached the far wall and began to feel about for the door. If the procession had already started Bir Beg would have gone, too. In that event he might get a free passage through the house into the bazaar outside, and even yet be at Winfield's bungalow in time to lie up for Mahomet Khan's attack on the catafalque.

He found the door, and to his immense relief it was still open. Stumbling inside, he felt about for the ladder which he remembered led up to the trapdoor in the ceiling. Presently his searching fingers encountered it, and, feeling for the bottom rung with his foot, he mounted carefully through the darkness.

Arrived at the top of the ladder he bunched himself beneath the trapdoor and listened intently, but everything was silent as the grave. He tried the trap tentatively, and it gave to his pressure. He pushed it a little higher. Now his eyes were on a level with the floor of the room, and a single glance round showed him that no one was there. Brilliant sunlight was streaming in through a latticed window, and beyond, the heartening murmur of the bazaar.

Satisfied, Blake thrust back the trapdoor and climbed out into the room. Save for a huddle of blankets in one corner the place was empty. Bir Beg had flown. Even now he was trailing his bait along the road to the pass. Even now Mahomet Khan might have attacked and succeeded in regaining his own.

He made for the door leading into the street but paused at sight of a black-looking stain seeping from beneath that huddle of blankets. He looked at it closer. It was blood. He lifted the top blankets and stared.

There was a man lying there—a dead man. He was lying on his face, and from the back of his neck protruded the hilt of a knife. Blake turned him over—and the next second literally froze in his tracks.

It was Bir Beg!

Bir Beg! Murdered—and already cold. Bir Beg— whom a moment ago he had thought to be on his way to the border.

Blake looked at him. The man had been dead for hours. He looked at his arrogant mouth now rigid and drawn; at the massive frame of him.

And as he stood there thinking a curious light crept into the detective's eyes. It was not Bir Beg's men who had knocked him out last night, because Bir Beg must himself have been dead by that time, and his game already lost. It was Mahomet Khan he had to thank for his aching head and his chafed wrists.

Mahomet Khan! The man he wanted for the murder of young Newman.

It was Mahomet Khan who had laid him out!

And, by the same token, Mahomet Khan was now in possession again of whatever it was he had brought out from England in those bales. He had struck before his time. He had won through before anyone had expected him to put in an appearance. And unless Winfield had stopped him on the way, he would by now be over the Abbabi Pass and in the safety of his own country.

Blake literally leapt for the door. There was not a moment to lose. He did not pause to see where he was. He turned left and ran swiftly through the bazaar until he found an ekka.

"Police sahib's bungalow!" he directed the driver. "Five rupees backsheesh if you get there in fifteen minutes!"

The driver lashed up his horse, and they were away— scattering the crowds as they went.

.   .   .   .   .

Judy Kershaw sprang to her feet when a startled servant announced Sexton Blake sahib.

"Don't let my appearance disturb you, Miss Kershaw," the detective apologised the moment he saw her. "I didn't expect to find you here. Is Tinker about?"

She looked at him blankly.

"I thought he was with you, Mr. Blake."

"You mean——"

She shook her head.

"He hasn't been back since he went out with you last night."

Blake put a hand to his aching head. In the full light of day he appeared weak and spent, although his eyes were as bright as ever.

"Ali Singh?" he asked a moment later.

"Neither of them, Mr. Blake."

Blake thought for a moment. They must still be down in the bazaar somewhere—bound, perhaps. Helpless. Mahomet Khan must have got the three of them.

"Has the procession gone?" he asked swiftly.

"Hours ago!"

"Did Winfield go out to look in the catafalque?"

"Yes, he went out this morning." She glanced at the clock. "Four hours ago now."

"Alone?"

"Yes. He daren't take anyone with him because of the sacrilege of it all."

Blake muttered an imprecation under his breath. Everything had gone wrong—everything!

"Bir Beg's dead!" he flung out bitterly. "It's Mahomet Khan who's running the show now."

Judy's hand flew to her throat. At last she understood.

"I knew that catafalque was a trap!" she cried. "Those men were not Bir Beg's men at all, they were Mahomet Khan's. That fat fakir was recognised by the havildar as being a friend of Mahomet Khan's—the one who was hanged."

Blake jerked upright. That fat fakir again? Friend of that other Mahomet Khan? Friend of this Mahomet Khan?

"Blind!" he ejaculated bitterly. "Blind we've been— all of us! And I blindest of all! Who's in charge of the police here?" he rapped out urgently.

She told him.

"Tell him to turn out every man he's got—armed and ready for action. And a horse for me, too, Miss Kershaw! I don't want to startle you, but it's neck or nothing now. Unless we can stop Mahomet Khan before he crosses the border, you'll lose a husband and I shall lose my assistant."

"What d'you mean?" she cried, her face paling till it was like a sheet.

"They're in that catafalque—both of them! That was the trap. That's what they're scheming for. Hurry up with those horses!"

It was typical of Judy Kershaw that she asked no questions. She simply leapt through the open french window and went racing away to the police lines. Within six minutes Blake had changed into riding-kit and the whole party was galloping up the road towards Abbabi Pass. And since she would not be left behind, Judy Kershaw rode with them.

Eight miles out they found the D.S.P.'s horse hobbled in a nullah beside a deep defile. In the dust of the road they saw the marks of many milling feet—also the marks where both catafalque and palanquin had been put down to rest. Blake read the signs accurately, and the line between his brows deepened.

"Hurry!" he urged. "Hurry!"

CHAPTER 16

THE FAKIR'S HOSTAGE

CAPTAIN James Winfield awoke to a curious swaying motion. In a vague kind of way he had been aware of it for some little time past, but now he opened his eyes to investigate. His first impression was that the world had grown suddenly blood-red; then someone spoke to him.

"Awake at last, captain?"

From the black pit of oblivion, Winfield struggled slowly upwards. He had heard that voice somewhere before. He steadied himself and looked up. Opposite him was the round face of the fat fakir, and the man was still smiling.

Winfield stared, and of a sudden his senses came back to him. He was sitting in the palanquin with the fakir. It was the fakir who had spoken to him. That redness was occasioned by the sun shining through the saffron curtains of the palanquin, and the swaying motion was imparted by the movements of the carriers underneath. He tried to ask what was the meaning of it all, but he found that he was gagged and bound and a helpless prisoner.

"You wake up too late to say goodbye to your home, captain."

Winfield considered that fat face. He did not quite appreciate what the man meant. He was struggling with a sense of almost ridiculous unreality.

"What's the game?" he wanted to ask. "You must be crazy to think you can kidnap a District Superintendent of Police like this and get away with it!" The thing was monstrous. It was absolutely unheard of. He eyed the fakir with rising fury.

The fellow smiled as though guessing his thoughts.

"You warned me to be across the border by sunset, captain," he said. "And, by Allah, we shall be so."

Winfield grew very white. He looked at the man again, conscious of an overwhelming desire to sink his fingers in that fat throat, to knock the mocking smile from that vast, moonlike face. And then he remembered that other face he had seen, back there in the defile. It came to him suddenly; the last thing he had seen before that blow on the head had knocked him senseless.

Blake's assistant—Tinker! It was Tinker he had seen in the catafalque. Tinker, bound cheek by jowl with the murdered Abdul Aza. Tinker—with a great gag in his mouth.

The memory seared his brain. In a spasm of ungovernable fury he tore at his bonds until the palanquin rocked with his efforts and the carriers below shouted out oaths and curses at him. But he might have been a fly struggling in a spider's web for all the notice the fat fakir took of him. Then he began to feel like a fly. He began to see the fakir as a fat, hairless spider into whose web he had fallen. That moist mouth, so round and flabby—he shook himself back to reason. He was losing his nerve. Was acting like a child.

"Many sahibs have I known, captain," the fakir chuckled insultingly, "but always have I found them fools."

"You fat ape!" Winfield tried to shout through his gag, but he might just as well not have made the effort for all the result he achieved. That gag was sound-proof.

The palanquin swayed on in silence for a time. What had happened, where they were or what it was, Winfield had no means of knowing. Only by the fading brilliance of the light coming through the saffron curtains could he guess that the day was dying and that they must be perilously near to the border. Again and again he racked his brains in an effort to think why they wanted him in that palanquin, but nothing he could think of seemed reasonable.

"What did you believe we had in that catafalque, captain?" the fakir asked presently. And when Winfield merely glared at him: "You see only what you are intended to see, captain," the man went on mockingly. "Hear only what you are intended to hear. You think we carry guns in that catafalque—but no! No, by Allah! One small bait and one piece of carrion meat—that is all we carry in our catafalque. Now, owing to obliging nature of Captain Winfield of Police—now we have our second piece of bait in this palanquin!"

He broke into a laugh that to Winfield fell smartingly as salt upon an open wound. He fairly writhed in his humiliation. Sitting there helpless and impotent, he could have cut his throat for the fool he had been. They had laid a trap for him, and he had walked into it like the biggest fool in Christendom.

Yet even now he could not see what they wanted him for. There were no guns in the catafalque—he knew that! He had known it before the fakir had spoken; he had seen as much with his own eyes. And of what use was Tinker to them that they should risk their lives for the sake of kidnapping him? Of what use was he himself, for that matter? There were dozens of other D.S.P.'s in India ready to take his place.

"Bait," the fakir had said. Judy had used the same word—bait for what? What was it the fakir was out to catch? And with whom was he working? Who had slit Abdul Aza's throat, and why? And why was his body in the catafalque?

He gave it up. "A good man with his hands but not of much use with his head," they had said of him at Sandhurst. Perhaps they were right. Perhaps he would have been wiser to remain with the regiment. Perhaps he really hadn't the brains to deal with this class of cunning and subtlety.

After that, his weary mind must have sunk into a state of coma, for when next he became aware of anything the inside of the palanquin was almost dark and the fakir was leaning over him peering out through the curtains at his back. The fat face was loathsomely near his own. The smell of betel nut was almost overpowering. He closed his eyes for a moment to shut out the hateful sight, but when he opened them again the fakir was still there.

He wondered what the man was looking at, and it came to him suddenly that the fat face reflected an anxious mind. There was apprehension in the pig-like eyes; uncertainty in the fat jaw. Something was happening behind that was not strictly according to plan, and Winfield's heart gave a sudden leap. Anything wrong for the fat fakir could only mean something equally right for himself!

He made a stupendous effort to wrench himself round.

"Be still!" snarled the fakir. He whipped a knife from beneath his robe and held it menacingly against Winfield's throat. "A party of your accursed police are coming up behind," he said. "That woman is with them, too, by Allah!" He broke off sharply, and across his face swept a look of indescribable malignity. "One day, captain, that woman will ride once too often this way!" he said. "Once—too—often, captain!"

But Winfield was not listening to the fakir. His ears were strained for the first thud of hoofs.

"Move as much as a finger while they are passing," the fakir warned him. His eyes were like pebbles in the gloom. His mouth was little better than a thin, straight line.

Winfield froze. The edge of that knife was like a white-hot wire across his throat, and he knew for a certainty that the fakir would send it shearing through sinew and muscle without a second thought if he considered that the occasion demanded it.

The horses were coming up rapidly. Suddenly he felt the fakir stiffen and curse, and the next second Winfield knew a blazing hope.

"That thrice-cunning dog of an English detective is there!" the fakir snarled. "By Allah, I warned my master that the dog would be safer dead!"

Winfield thrilled to his words. If Sexton Blake were out there, surely a rescue would be affected!

He listened intently, the blood drumming loudly in his ears. By the jingle of bits and accoutrements, the entire available force must be there. His agonised eyes fixed themselves on the saffron curtains. Every second he expected to see a hand come through, but nothing happened. No one challenged.

Were they going to miss him? Were they going to ride past and leave him to his fate? Sweat oozed from his forehead and trickled down his face. Only a thin curtain between himself and life, and not a solitary hand to tear it aside.

The blood was hammering madly in his temples. If only he could shout. If only he could signal them in some way. But his bonds held him fast, and he could not force even a whisper through that gag. And always that fat fakir held the knife hard against his windpipe.

But they were riding past. They were going on. They had not seen him. They did not know he was there.

They were past!

He fell to frenzy. He became quite mad. Above him,

the fakir's face swelled to gigantic proportions, and the knife bit like a live thing at his throat, but he scarcely felt it. Nothing mattered now if only he could let them know he was there.

Suddenly one of the bearers down below cried out on a note of fear. The palanquin swayed dangerously. There was another cry. The front of the palanquin fell down with a crash, shooting out the fakir as it fell.

The next thing Winfield knew, he was lying flat on his back in the dust.

"He's all right," he heard Judy saying in Hindustani. "Cut that stuff from his mouth, havildar, and send someone to get the flask from my saddlebag."

"That—fakir!" he gasped from between tortured jaws.

"They've gone after him now," she assured him. "He bolted into that nullah—I doubt if they'll find him in this light."

She gave him something to drink, and he felt better. Presently he struggled upright. Immediately in front of him was the wrecked palanquin, and a little way behind he could just make out the shape of the big catafalque lying broken on its side.

"Tinker!" he jerked out suddenly. "Tinker's in the catafalque!"

She nodded her head.

"Mr. Blake thought he would be," she smiled. "He's with him now. He's all right."

Then she told him what had happened.

"Mr. Blake wasn't absolutely sure how you would be fixed—but he guessed the fakir would try to hold you as a hostage for his own safety. That was why he would not allow the havildar to challenge him. He thought it best that I rode you down. I pretended that my horse was out of control as I passed you. I lifted him on his hind legs and brought him down plumb across the shafts of the palanquin. The carriers bolted, of course, and the whole thing crashed over sideways. Unfortunately, the fakir was shot free as it fell, and almost before he had touched the ground he was up again and into that nullah. I've never seen a man move so fast in my life. I'm afraid he'll get away in the gloom."

Winfield looked across the plain to where several of his men were riding this way and that, but Judy's fears were well founded. It was dusk, even on the plain—and with the nullahs running to as much as forty feet deep, twisting and turning in all directions, honey-combed with holes and natural caves, and connected one with another by hundreds of narrow, tortuous channels, the advantage was all with the pursued.

"But I'll get him!" Winfield said between his teeth. "I'll get that fakir if it's the last thing I ever do!"

CHAPTER 17

THE RIDER FROM FAMIPUR

YOUTH is notoriously resilient. Within a quarter of an hour of being freed from his bonds, Tinker was more or less his usual, smiling self. And at a bound he was on the job again.

"Guv'nor," he reported the instant his aching jaws could be persuaded to function, "I believe I heard Mahomet Khan last night. At any rate, someone spoke to me in an Oxford accent."

"Where?" Blake ripped out.

"I don't know where it was. I was tied up in a blanket at the time, I couldn't see—but I heard him all right. It was just after someone had slit a hole in the blanket over my mouth and made me drink something that tasted like butyl chloride."

"Seems to make a speciality of that!" Blake murmured. "Go on?"

"I didn't drink any more than I was forced to, guv'nor, and it didn't have much effect. But after they'd given it to me, this chap came up and said: 'Sleep well, Mr.

Tinker!'—just like that. It sounded as though he were amused. 'Sleep well, Mr. Tinker!' he said. That was after they'd knocked me out."

"Where did that happen?"

"In the bazaar. But it was in a house that he spoke to me. They must have carried me there, though I don't remember it. That house was where the procession started from because when they lifted me into the catafalque it wasn't more than half a dozen steps away. Where did the procession start from?"

"Bir Beg's house, I imagine," Blake said. And then: "Did you hear his voice at all—Bir Beg's, I mean?"

"No. I heard that fat fakir's, though—the fellow who brought Mr. Winfield to the catafalque this afternoon, and then knocked him on the head."

"When did you hear him?"

"He helped to lift me into the catafalque, guv'nor."

"How long had you been conscious before then?"

Tinker thought for a minute.

"On and off, ever since daylight," he said at last.

"And in all that time you never once heard the voice of Bir Beg?"

"Not once! I'm sure I'd have known it if I had."

Blake smiled. That confirmed a very curious suspicion which for hours past had been taking shape in his brain.

"Tell me exactly what happened after I left you at the well," he said presently. "You were joined there by Ali Singh, I believe?"

"That's right. Is he all right, by the way? I left him facing up to about a dozen of 'em there—he's a good man, Ali Singh!"

Blake nodded. He related how he had sent Ali Singh to stop the police coming. He had not seen him since.

"Reckon the same mob got him in the bazaar as got me," Tinker mused. "Like enough made a job of it with him."

He went on to tell how Ali Singh had called to him

from the silversmith's shop, and how the two of them had mounted guard together over the well top.

"He had followed us from the bungalow, guv'nor—had Major Christie's orders, apparently, to keep an eye on us. Anyway, we sat down there together and waited for you to come back. Then—it might have been half an hour later—we heard sounds coming from the silversmith's shop, and before we had a chance to hide ourselves, out rushed Bir Beg, Verislov, and about half a dozen other ruffians. I fired into the thick of 'em, and one man fell, but it was obvious at once that we couldn't hope to hold that little lot! Ali Singh called to me to get over the wall and run for assistance; they wouldn't harm him, he said, since he would say that he was only my servant. I did that. It seemed to be the only possible thing. But as I ran through the bazaar, three natives leapt out at me, armed with lathis. I hadn't a chance. The next thing I knew, I was lying on my back, gagged and blind-folded, on a pile of blankets."

"In a corner?" Blake asked.

"That's right, guv'nor."

So they had kept him in Bir Beg's house? Blake thought as much. It fitted in exactly with his theory. They had knocked Tinker on the head and taken him to Bir Beg's house. Later on, Mahomet Khan had taken control of the place and used Tinker to the best advantage.

He related his own adventures down the well, finishing up with his discovery of the dead body of Bir Beg.

"My gosh!" Tinker said at the end of it all. "He's a holy terror, this Mahomet Khan bloke. Was it he who got Verislov?"—nodding to where the body of the silversmith lay just as it had fallen from the overturned catafalque.

"For revenge," Blake said.

"And who got Bir Beg?"

Blake was silent for a moment.

"Mahomet Khan himself got Bir Beg," he said quietly. "Now, then, shall we go and see how Winfield is shaping?"

They found the D.S.P. already on his feet. In a few

words he related everything that had happened in the palanquin.

"But the swine's got away," he fumed. "He'll be safe across the border by moonrise."

"Or back in Famipur," Blake said.

"What?"

"Back in Famipur," Blake repeated. "He hasn't finished his job there yet."

Winfield stared at the detective as though he had taken leave of his senses.

"Back in Famipur?" he echoed. "After this little lot?"

Blake smiled.

"He hasn't finished his job yet, I tell you," he explained quietly. "That fat fakir is Mahomet Khan's righthand man, and they're working together for big stakes. The object of all these preparations is two-fold—firstly to secure from Bir Beg what he stole from those bales, and secondly, to get that same stuff across the border. Their first object they have already achieved. Bir Beg is lying dead in his house, and Mahomet Khan is once again in possession of whatever it was he put in those bales in Tanner & Wild's warehouse. The second object they will attend to immediately."

"But——"

"Listen!" Blake said on a sharper note. "Everything that has happened up to date is merely the prelude to what is going to happen tonight. That fakir referred to you as 'bait'—he was right. You were bait. You were one bait, and Tinker was the other. And both of you were intended for the same purpose—namely, to open the Pass for Mahomet Khan tonight."

"To run those guns?" Winfield gasped.

"There are no guns!" Blake told him. "We're too late for those. The guns from that dump were taken over months ago, and are now securely hidden in Mahomet's own country——"

"What?"

"Months ago," Blake repeated, waving aside the

D.S.P.'s incredulous exclamation. "The stuff we are dealing with now is the stuff that Mahomet Khan brought out from England in those bales—and that is what he is going to run through the Pass tonight."

"But, my God, man, how do you know all——"

"Never mind that now," Blake cut him short. "I do know it. Mahomet Khan has cut across Bir Beg's plans to remove that stuff in the catafalque. Bir Beg planned to remove the stuff just as you thought—in the catafalque, that is. But Mahomet Khan knew that you were going to look into that catafalque, so he had to revise the scheme. He decided to turn his knowledge to the best advantage, so he let the affair go through as planned by Bir Beg, with the sole exception of putting the stuff inside. Instead of doing that, he determined to use the catafalque as bait, and run the stuff across later on, when he had cleared the Pass of police."

"But——"

"Just think for a moment," Blake went on. "Imagine the consternation among your havildars when they found you missing. Immediately they would have sounded the SOS and put on every man in the force to look for you. Pass, border, frontier—everything would have been forgotten in the frantic search for you. And the same with Tinker. Mahomet Khan knew that I should turn the bazaar inside out until I found him—and that would keep me occupied and away from the Pass. The whole affair was planned to that one end, Winfield, to draw back the watch from the Pass, and so give Mahomet Khan a free passage across the border for himself and his loot."

He paused. Judy Kershaw was watching him with shining eyes, but the D.S.P. was clearly still all at sea.

It was Tinker who broke the long silence.

"But if this fat fakir has escaped," he said, "and gone back to Famipur to warn Mahomet Khan that his plan has failed—how then?"

"That's where we've got to look out for trouble," Blake agreed. "The point is this: now that he knows that we are aware of his scheme and his hiding-place, he dare not delay. He knows very well that in spite of cut wires and all the rest of it, Winfield will get news through to head-quarters. He knows that by tomorrow morning every available man will be centred about Famipur and that tunnel. He knows that before midday tomorrow re-inforcements will be arriving from down-country to hold the Pass in even greater force than it's held now. Unless he is safely over the border before daylight tomorrow he'll never get over at all. He'll be caught like a rat in a trap, and in that event he'll lose everything he's striven for—even to his life. We're on his heels, and he knows it. It's now or never for him—and he'll make it now! Tonight, that is."

Winfield woke up with a jerk. Here was something he really did understand.

"You mean he'll try to run that stuff tonight?" he asked excitedly.

"I can't see that he has any option in the matter."

"You mean he will run it tonight?"

"He'll have to run it tonight—or not at all."

"Then we've got him cold!" In a moment Winfield was bubbling over with confidence. Now he knew what was expected of him. Now he saw what he had to do. If it was a matter of holding the border against all comers until daylight tomorrow, Captain James Winfield was the man to do it!

His cocksuredness made Blake shudder. He knew that things would not work out as easily as all that.

"It will be a battle of wits rather than of rifles," he felt impelled to warn the D.S.P. "Mahomet Khan knows you will be here in force, and he is not the man to walk into such a trap with his eyes open. And they will be open—make no mistake about that! He'll try every trick in his basket to draw you out of position."

But James Winfield merely smiled. He had a high opinion of Blake's brains and strategy, but when it came to fighting the frontier, that was his department! It would take a better man than Mahomet Khan to dislodge him from a position, once he had dug himself in.

"I'll send you back with an escort," he said to Judy as he set about making his arrangements. "I shall have to send back to barracks, in any case." He gave three short blasts on his whistle for the havildar, and when the man came running up he was met with such a spate of instructions as made Blake realise that, slow as Winfield was in some directions, when it came to his own job—soldiering —he was right in the top class. Four men were to guard the rest-house, in case any marauder should take it into his head to do a little thieving while the police were away—but every other available man was to come up to the Pass. Food and water were to be brought up, sufficient for the entire force for the night, extra ammunition, signalling-lamps, a torch for himself—he thought of everything.

"Are we staying here?" Tinker asked Blake as Judy and her escort prepared to ride away.

Blake nodded.

"Yes," he said. "That lad's a bit too impetuous for my liking. At present the cards are all in our hands; but unless they're played carefully we shall lose the game even yet."

Meanwhile, with Judy gone, Winfield set about making his preparations. Headquarters he decided to establish in the road at the mouth of the Pass, and the foothills to right and left would be suitably picketed. His main body he decided to hold in reserve in the Pass. Every single nullah running at right angles to the border—any nullah along which anyone could creep—was to be stopped at its mouth with a picket, and wing posts, supplied with signalling-lamps, were flung out some half mile forward across the plain.

By nine o'clock the party had returned from the barracks and everything was ready. And when, at ten o'clock, Blake accompanied him round the various posts, he was satisfied that not even a rat could get through the defences without being spotted. Then they sat down to wait.

CHAPTER 18

BLAKE SPRINGS A SURPRISE

An hour passed—a second hour. Nothing stirred. By now the moon was riding high overhead, so that the plain lay stretched out like a shimmering, misty sea.

Blake sat, chin in hand, on the warm sand, thinking. The loneliness, the vastness, the stark barrenness of the frontier landscape reminded him of a picture he had seen long ago, purporting to be a scene on the moon. There was the same fantastic grandeur, the same suggestion of stillness, of immeasurable age.

As time passed, and nothing happened, the intense silence began to get on Winfield's nerves. He began to wriggle about, to worry.

"You're sure they haven't made for the eastern pass?" he asked Blake for the fiftieth time.

The detective shook his head. The eastern pass was sixty miles away, and to reach that Mahomet Khan would have to travel by day. He wouldn't risk such a journey. It wasn't reasonable.

"But it isn't reasonable to suppose that, knowing we're here, he'll come this way!" the D.S.P. argued. He was getting nervy and jumpy. Was he sitting there like a fool while Mahomet Khan and his men were running their loot elsewhere? Had that fat fakir made contact with his master and hatched out some other cunning scheme?

A gnawing doubt began to undermine his belief in Blake's efficiency. It crept upon him unawares, born of the silence and the waiting. Why should Mahomet Khan come this way, when he knew that the entire police force of the district was sitting up for him? The guns from that mysterious arms dump were already lost to them—were they to lose this bales case as well? They were wasting time. They were sitting there like fools, while Mahomet Khan and his men were racing towards the eastern pass.

He sprang suddenly to his feet, alarm bells ringing loudly in his ears. The plain was as bare as the back of his hand. Not a thing was moving anywhere. It was absurd! Blake had made a mistake. Mahomet Khan was not coming this way.

"Havildar!" he called sharply to the sergeant sitting in front of him.

"It is a horse, huzoor!" the man whispered. "I have been listening to it for some little time past. It is coming up the road."

"Galloping, too!" Blake added quietly.

"Galloping?" Winfield almost gasped the word. If anyone were galloping openly along that road, it could only mean one thing.

"They've gone the other way!" he cursed furiously. "They've made for the eastern pass. I told you they would!"

He could hear the horse himself now. Could even see it, emerging from the misty moonlight. He ran down to the road, Blake following him.

"Who is it?" Tinker asked.

"I don't know." Blake stared ahead into the pale mist, seeing nothing but a white blur. Suddenly he stiffened. "It's the doctor!" he rapped out on a note of amazement. "It's Dr. Kershaw!"

The breath caught cold in Winfield's throat. An awful presentiment shook him from head to heel. Forgetting concealment, Mahomet Khan, loot and everything, he ran out to meet the oncoming horseman. Now he could see for himself that it was Dr. Kershaw. He was riding Judy's big stallion, Akbar the Great. He would know the horse among a thousand.

"What's the matter?" he called out as he ran. "What's happened, doctor?"

Dr. Kershaw pulled up the great horse and literally fell

from his back. Horror was in his eyes. His face was white as a sheet; he could scarcely speak.

"Judy!" he gasped. "They've stolen her, Winfield. She's gone!"

"Judy?"

"She's gone!"

Blake caught the old doctor's arm.

"Steady, man—steady!" he said. "What has happened, exactly?"

"They must have crept up in the dark. Two of the guards are dead, the other two unconscious. They pulled Judy out of bed. I heard her scream and rushed in, but a fat man kicked me in the stomach—I was helpless. I hadn't time to get my revolver. It was all over in a minute."

"Where did they go?"

"They told me—through the bazaar. I don't know. I came straight here." Suddenly the doctor lost what little self-control he had left. "You oughtn't to have left us down there without proper protection!" he raved at Winfield. "It's your fault. Get after them! Bring her back! And bring me that fat brute so that I can choke him with my bare hands! Oh, Judy——"

He began to rave and tear his hair. He was plainly all in. Blake tried to calm him, but it was useless.

"Guv'nor," Tinker said suddenly, "they've fired the bungalow—or the barracks!"

Blake turned sharply, and his eyes narrowed. A vast brightness was reflected in the sky in the direction of Famipur.

"It's the barracks!" he decided at once.

Then James Winfield came to life again. It seemed as though the news had stunned him for a moment, but now he leapt into frenzied activity.

"Sound the alarm, havildar!" he shouted. And as the havildar passed the word to the bugler and a muted blare brought even the farthest pickets leaping to their feet: "Up you get, doctor!" he cried. "We're going back at once!"

"Aren't you leaving a guard here?" Blake asked.

"What? With Judy missing and Mahomet Khan racing for the eastern pass—not likely! I shall want every man and every rifle I can muster before we're through with this packet!"

The men were already getting to horse. Blake hesitated for a moment, then went off to his own mount.

"Is it a trap?" Tinker asked as they ran.

But for once even Sexton Blake was uncertain. In any event they would have to go after Miss Kershaw.

Ten minutes later the entire party was mounted and galloping south again. Dr. Kershaw was mouthing hate and black curses, but Winfield rode with a set face and unsteady hands. Fooled and fooled yet again—that had been his history for the day.

Now they had got Judy!

. . . . .

When eventually they arrived in cantonments they found themselves confronted with a heap of glowing ash that had once been the police lines. A great crowd had assembled from the native city, men, women and children, who all started shouting at once. They were excited and frightened. Never had such a thing happened within living memory. Each had a tale to tell, but Winfield pushed through them and went straight to his office.

He tried the telephone, but the line was still dead. Then he began to bawl for information, for anyone who had seen the swine—but Blake stepped past him and himself took command. He instructed the havildar to bring in the head men of the city, or anyone else who had reliable information to give.

"I'm not trying to interfere with your department, Winfield," he apologised, "but Mahomet Khan belongs to me, and I want him."

"You want him?" Winfield laughed shortly. "By God, Blake, when I've finished with him there'll be nothing left for you—or the hangman!" he added.

Blake shrugged. He could make all due allowance for the D.S.P.'s state of mind, but he was playing his own game and he meant to win.

"First we've got to catch him," he said grimly as the havildar returned with his first witness.

He was a man from Famipur City. He had seen the robbers pass. The glow in the sky had brought him hot-foot to the sahib's bungalow. Bad men were everywhere, he said.

"You actually saw the memsahib?" Blake asked.

"Aie, huzoor. A fat fakir had her across his saddle."

"How do you know it was the memsahib?"

"I saw her, huzoor. Her boots, her clothes, her helmet —everything!"

"That's good enough!" Winfield interrupted brusquely. "Let's get going, Blake!"

But the detective shook his head. Dr. Kershaw had said that his daughter had been taken from her bed—then why the breeches, boots and helmet? He called for Tinker.

"Run over to the rest-house and find out if any of Miss Kershaw's clothes have been taken," he said. "Particularly boots and helmet."

He turned to the man again.

"Had they anything else with them?" he asked.

"Many men carrying loads, huzoor. Guns, they said they were. Stutter-guns."

"Stutter-guns?"

"Machine-guns!" Winfield burst out in a sudden blaze of understanding. "By heavens, Blake, you were wrong after all! That dump hasn't been cleared! They're clearing it now! They're taking both Judy and guns through the eastern pass, and——"

"Wait a minute!" Blake rapped out shortly. He addressed himself to the man again. "How do you know they were stutter-guns?" he asked.

"They said so, huzoor—those men. They were laughing and talking about it."

"There you are, you see!" Winfield thrust in excitedly. "Does that satisfy you? Will you start now?"

"No." Blake voice was like a rapier to the other's bludgeon. He dismissed the man and called for the next. That one came from a village outside the city boundary, and from him Blake learned that the party was travelling eastwards at a fast pace. They had stopped for water in that village, and the headman had stood as close to the memsahib in the darkness as he was to Blake now.

He was still speaking when a sudden commotion in the doorway drowned his voice. Another man was trying to push past the havildar to get into the office.

"The sahib knows me!" he was shouting wildly. "I am an old constable—the sahib knows me, I tell you!"

"Let him come in!" Blake called.

The havildar stood aside, and the man literally fell into the room. He was in a bad way—sweating at every pore and obviously terrified.

"Sahib, I have seen a bhut!" he shrilled. "A bhut!"

"Get out!" Winfield cursed him. The fellow was crazy. "Get out!" he snarled.

But Blake gestured the man to stay.

"What ghost have you seen, constable?" he asked in a curiously tense voice.

The fellow turned to him as one turns to a saviour.

"Huzoor!" he panted. "I am not drunk. I am not mad. I am not blind. Eighteen months ago I saw a man taken in dacoitry. I saw that man hanged, huzoor. Hanged!" he screamed. "Yet tonight I saw that man again. He rode through my village, huzoor. He was riding furiously. He said no word, huzoor—but the moon was in his eyes and I knew him for that man I had seen hanged for dacoitry. It is written that the dead come not back, huzoor, but I——"

"Get out!" Winfield stormed. "You're drunk, you old fool!"

"On the contrary," Blake contradicted with his thinnest smile, "the man is obviously sober. Moreover, he is telling the truth." He turned again to the perspiring constable. "Whose ghost did you see?" he asked.

"The ghost of that Saiyid chief, huzoor!" the man gasped. "Mahomet Khan—the man I saw hanged!"

.   .   .   .   .

A dead silence greeted his statement. Then Winfield laughed.

"Rot!" he said shortly. "That's nonsense. The man was hanged by a subaltern of my own regiment——"

"He was not!" Blake cut in without hesitation. "I've known that for some little time past now. How the mistake occurred I can't imagine; but I do know that the Saiyid chief you 'hanged', and the fellow who murdered young Newman in London, is one and the same man. It couldn't be otherwise."

"But——"

"Yes, I know it sounds impossible, but it is true. It must be true! No other explanation fits the facts of the case. That Saiyid chief was not hanged—couldn't have been. He's alive today, and he is the man I want for the murder of young Newman. It was he who ordered the arms from Verislov in the first case, and he who helped form that dump in Peshawar. It was he who later on rifled that dump! It was he who ran the guns from that dump to their present hiding-place across the border, and he who brought out those bales. Incidentally, it is he who is at the back of kidnapping Miss Kershaw—— Yes?" he broke off as Tinker clattered into the room.

"They've taken her clothes," the young detective reported. "Breeches, boots, shirt and helmet—all are missing."

Winfield leapt to his feet.

"That settles that, then!" he cried. "Now we've got 'em cold, Blake! From here to the eastern pass is every bit of sixty miles, and while they are on foot—laden down with loot, not to mention Judy—we're well mounted and comparatively fresh. For every mile they cover, we can cover six! And by the look of things, they can't be more than a couple of hours ahead of us. Are you ready?"

"Yes!" With sudden decision Blake jumped to his feet. He whispered to Tinker as they followed the D.S.P. outside, and Tinker nodded.

"They're making for the eastern pass!" Winfield shouted to his havildar as he swung himself into his saddle. "We shall have him by daylight!"

Now they were up and away. Straight through the bazaar they rode, through the villages beyond and out into the open country. For six miles they continued their mad career, then Blake reined back and compelled the column to halt.

"We stop here," he said to Winfield. "We've come far enough to deceive any spies who might have been in that crowd. Now we're going back."

"Back where?" Winfield ripped out after a second's amazed silence.

"Abbabi Pass!" said Sexton Blake.

CHAPTER 19

THE FAT FAKIR

For a full minute the two men sat eyeing each other in the gloom. Then with a sudden movement Winfield's hand shot down to his holster.

"Get out of my way, Blake!" he said quietly, his voice plumb on the danger-line. "Stand aside and let my men pass."

"No!" Blake leaned forward, and his hand descended upon the other's wrist in a grip of steel. "This is a trap, my dear fellow. Just another trick that Mahomet Khan has pulled from his basket. If Mahomet Khan had intended escaping by the eastern pass, what would he need beyond everything else in the world?—time, wouldn't he? He would need time—as much start as he

could get. His sole hope of ever reaching the eastern pass
would be to creep out of Famipur like a mouse and ride
like hell through the night, avoiding every village and
every house on his way.

"And he had the chance to do that, Winfield! He had
that chance. With every available policeman sitting tight
on the border he had that chance. But does he take it?
Not he! Instead, he starts raising Cain in the place—
why? Is that the action of a clever man—of a man with a
kingdom at stake?"

He paused. His words were having the desired effect.
In spite of himself Winfield was listening.

"Consider what those men told us," Blake went on
again. "Had you been Mahomet Khan, having stolen a
white woman, and being laden down with loot, would you
ride through the bazaar proclaiming your name and
business and the fact that you were carrying machine-
guns—which, incidentally, he isn't! Would it be your
object to blaze a trail behind you as broad as the wake of a
ship? Would you have dressed Miss Kershaw in breeches
and boots—even a helmet—to proclaim to every half-
witted villager that you had kidnapped a white woman?
Of course you wouldn't! You'd have travelled along the
by-roads and as soon as possible taken to the open
country, covering your tracks as you went—because
you'd want all the time you could get! And you'd have
thrown a native robe over Miss Kershaw's European
clothes!

"Mahomet Khan is no fool, Winfield, as his history
ought to show you. He knows he could never make the
eastern pass without being intercepted—must know it!
He couldn't make it in the time unless he had at least
eight hours' start—and that he deliberately throws away.
Let me tell you something else. The man you knew as
Abdul Aza was actually a Russian named Paul Verislov.
He was the most notorious gun-runner in the trade, and
he was the man who supplied those original arms to
Mahomet Khan. They had trouble, now Mahomet

Khan has slit the man's throat—as you know. But he's got what he wanted! He's got the loot from those bales, and he's sitting prettier than he's ever sat in his life before. He's got a kingdom in his hands—the power he has always sought. The guns in that dump were machine-guns—and he's got them all over the border. Now he's got what he brought out from England in those bales. All he wants is to get back to his own country—is he going to mess about stealing a white woman and firing a mere barracks for nothing better than the fun of doing it? Is that his character? Does it fit?

"No!" he answered himself. "It doesn't fit. But it fits with his real desire! He tried this afternoon to draw the police from Abbabi Pass by kidnapping you. That failed so he tries the same scheme all over again. Now he has stolen Miss Kershaw—knowing that nothing on earth would bring you down quicker than that! He knew the doctor would ride for help—that's why he didn't kill him then and there! But in case he failed to arrive, they fired the barracks—why? Simply and solely because we should see the glare on the sky and know that something was wrong.

"The whole thing is too obvious to miss," he went on more urgently. "Mahomet Khan has laid a trail that a fool could follow—and he thinks we are fools! He aimed to draw us from Abbabi Pass, as in fact, he has drawn us! Even now he is creeping across country with Miss Kershaw and the loot—and the pass is wide open to him. There isn't a soul to stop him, or to rescue Miss Kershaw. It's the same scheme all over again, Winfield—but this time, unless you trust me, they're going to win through. Which is it to be?"

Winfield had heard him out in silence. Throughout the long exposition he had said never a word, but his face was a study. He was torn by doubt and a horrible fear. Racked between the ice-cold logic of Sexton Blake and his own overwhelming desire to save the woman he loved.

"It's her life we're playing with!" he cried in agony.

F

"Her very life, Blake! If we make a mistake now, she's lost!"

"I know." The great detective's face was stern and hard. "I know that," he said again. "But if Miss Kershaw were my only daughter, I'd still make for Abbabi Pass. I pledge you my word, Winfield, that that's where you will find her."

The harassed man beat his brow. His eyes were the eyes of a hunted wild thing, not knowing which way to turn. For a full minute he hung in the balance, then, very suddenly as it seemed to Blake, he cracked.

"As you like," he said in a dead flat voice. "Let's go!"

He mounted his horse heavily, turned in his tracks, and struck off across country without a word, his men clattering along at his heels.

"Abbabi Pass!" Blake whispered to the astounded havildar as he rode past him to catch up with Winfield in the lead.

.   .   .   .   .

Striking off at right angles to the track—cautiously because of the dying moon and the nullahs—Winfield fetched a wide circle back to the frontier. Arriving at a deep nullah, at Blake's suggestion, he ordered the entire troop to dismount. He placed a guard over the horses, explained briefly what was afoot, and presently led his men scouting forward towards their old positions.

They arrived there two hours before dawn, and one by one sank noiselessly into the landscape. By now the moon had dropped behind the mountains so that the plain lay dark and mysterious beneath the paling stars. From his position at the mouth of the pass, Blake strained his ears to catch the slightest sound, but the world seemed utterly dead. Not a thing was moving anywhere.

Time passed swiftly, a quarter-hour, a half-hour, three-quarters, and still nothing stirred. Cold, cramped, with the dawn already in the wind, Winfield's spirits sank to zero. Was it possible that Sexton Blake had made a mistake? Was there something he had failed to take into account?

The thought made him sick with anxiety. If a mistake had been made this time, nothing in the world could ever put it right.

The wind had dropped now, and the stillness was intense. In a very short time it would be day. Already he thought he could discern a faint radiance in the eastern sky.

He heard a slight movement, and the next moment Sexton Blake crept up beside him.

"When they come," he said, "you mark the fat fakir. Leave Mahomet Khan to me—he's mine!"

Winfield nodded.

"You're—you're still sure they'll come?" he whispered, unable to bear the awful suspense.

"I think they must be quite near by now," Blake answered. "You won't forget about Mahomet Khan?"

Winfield shook his head. Give him a chance at that fat fakir, and that was all he asked of life at the moment.

"But you don't know Mahomet Khan!" he said suddenly. "I don't myself, for that matter. I never saw him."

"Nevertheless," Blake whispered, "I think I shall be able to pick him out." He paused for a moment, his eyes on the younger man's ravaged face. "It was Mahomet Khan who sent those two wires," he said then. "The ones you read for me—remember?"

"The one to Abdul Aza signed—what was it? Canary?"

"That's the one. He must have slipped a woman's purdah robe over his own clothes and passed himself off as a woman."

The detective chuckled, and crept back again to his own side of the road. He seemed in high good humour. Winfield heard him chuckling again with Tinker. Then silence fell.

Winfield strained his eyes across the darkened plain. He seemed to have been waiting for hours when suddenly he felt a touch on his arm.

His heart leapt.

"Yes?" he whispered to the native who had touched him. "Yes?"

"There are men coming up the road, huzoor. Many men, I think."

Winfield listened intently, but could hear nothing. He forced himself to stillness and waiting, though the effort made him sick. A rustle on his right warned him that his men had heard the sounds, too. They were closing in on the roads—moving softly, like grey shadows. Somewhere along the line a bolt snicked.

And now he could hear something himself. A vague shuffling movement, as of sandals dragging through thick dust.

Noiselessly he got to his feet, the havildar beside him. Judging by the nearness of the sounds, the leaders of the party must be already within the circle of his waiting police. The light in the east was strengthening rapidly. In a minute or two more it would be broad day.

He strained forward, his heart in his mouth. Three vague figures were emerging from the gloom. They came on steadily, their heads turned this way and that.

Scouts!

Winfield crouched farther behind the rock which hid him. A glance across the narrow road assured him that Blake and Tinker were alike invisible. Behind him the police had gone to earth as silently as rabbits. The trap was set.

The three scouts came on swiftly. They had done with the nullahs, and were now scanning the dizzy heights above the pass. They reached the mouth of the defile, paused for a moment, then plunged boldly into the gloom; but still Winfield gave no sign. Let them go through! They were carrying nothing save their own arms.

A few minutes more, and other figures loomed up out of the dusk—porters, this time, carrying the loot. Winfield counted twenty of them. Then, some ten yards behind, unmistakable even in the half light, came the fat fakir.

"Huzoor!" breathed the havildar suddenly. "Look, the missy-sahib!"

Winfield's jaws came together with an audible click. He, too, had seen that slight figure trailing along at the end of a rope behind the fat fakir. He, too, had seen. And, in spite of the native rags that covered her, he knew her for Judy Kershaw.

"Leave that hound to me!" he got out from between white lips. But he did not draw his revolver. The fat fakir was on his side of the road, and he knew exactly what he was going to do. The porters were already within the "pincers" of his men. Remained now only to give the signal and to square his account with the fat fakir.

Holding himself taut as a bowstring, he waited until the man was level with his hiding-place. He waited until he could see the whites of his eyes, then:

"Look out, Judy!" he roared.

The fakir spun round as though on a pivot—too late. Already Winfield was on top of him. Unleashing an uppercut that would have floored an elephant, Winfield caught him a sickening crack plump among those rolls of fat which decorated the fellow's throat, and he went down like a poleaxed bull. He never moved, never made a sound. Just as the first shot of the ambush whined up the pass, Winfield cut Judy free of her bonds and carried her to the side of the road.

"Stay there!" he said. "I'll be back in a minute or two."

The surprise was perfect, he saw. Twenty yards up the road the porters were huddled together like frightened sheep. One or two of the more daring ones had leapt for the precipitous sides, but those the police marksmen were picking off at leisure, like flies from a wall. Beyond, grotesque patches of black on the grey of the dusty road, lay the three scouts.

"Where's Blake?" he asked, coming upon Tinker in the scramble.

The young detective spat the dust from his mouth. His face was grey with the stuff.

"Gone to look for Mahomet Khan," he said. "He's not here."

"Hasn't he come?"

"No. Not unless he was behind the fat fakir when you slogged him. He didn't come into the pass."

"There was nobody behind the fakir, Tinker. He was the last man. Looks like he's dished you!"—and the D.S.P. ran on to connect up with his havildar in front.

Tinker went back to find his chief. He found the great detective leaning over the fakir, his eyes bitter with disappointment.

"Is he dead, guv'nor?" he asked, eyeing the thin trickle of blood that was oozing from the unconscious man's mouth.

"No, but he soon will be!" Blake snapped. "Winfield hit him harder than he knew, and since he is the only man who could tell me anything about Mahomet Khan——"

"What about Miss Kershaw?"

Blake snatched himself upright. Renewed hope shone brightly in his eyes.

"We can try her!" he agreed. "Come on!"

CHAPTER 20

WHAT THE BALES CONTAINED

THEY found the girl lying weak and spent behind a shelter of boulders. Blake looked at her cut and bleeding feet, at the filthy rags that covered her, and something like an oath ripped suddenly from his set lips.

Now he saw where they had fooled him! The absence of her clothes—breeches, boots, shirt, and helmet, told its own story. They had never taken her towards the eastern pass. Those villagers had lied. They had undoubtedly seen someone dressed in her clothes, but they had not seen Judy Kershaw!

Blake's eyes narrowed. Leaning over, he touched her gently. She opened her eyes and sat up, stared at him for a moment, then contrived a wry smile.

"Congratulations upon your escape, Miss Kershaw," Blake said. "Do you feel strong enough to talk?"

She nodded, and somewhat bashfully rearranged her rags. A moment later her eyes fell upon the unconscious fakir, and she shuddered.

"You got him, then?" she asked chokily.

Blake nodded.

"Winfield attended to that!" he said. "But the chief person we want is not here. I refer to Mahomet Khan. Can you tell me anything about him?"

"He's gone to the eastern pass, Mr. Blake."

"What!"

"Yes. He went off when the fakir came back. He's crossing there. I heard him say so. He must be nearly there by now."

For a moment even Sexton Blake was staggered.

"The eastern pass?" he echoed.

"Yes," she assured him. "He's laying the trail for you. He thinks you're still following him."

Blake grappled with his bewilderment. He had been up for forty-eight hours; perhaps his brain was wool-gathering.

"He left his precious loads to ride to the eastern pass?" he asked incredulously. Then he recovered himself. "Tell me exactly what happened, Miss Kershaw?" he asked crisply. "Begin at the beginning. What happened after they took you from the rest-house?"

Judy Kershaw collected her thoughts. Very briefly she related how she had awakened to find herself being dragged from bed by the fat fakir, and how he had taken her to a deep nullah where the Wardakis gang was assembled.

"Was Mahomet Khan there?" Blake interrupted.

She nodded.

"I didn't see him," she said, "but I heard him talking, and I heard them using his name. The nullah was very dark. It was impossible to see anyone clearly, but I would know his voice again if I heard it. It is a very soft voice, Mr. Blake—a cultured voice."

"I know it is!" Blake smiled bitterly. "But unfortunately he has another voice, and that's the only one I've managed to hear up to now. Go on!"

"Well, the fakir said he had a score to settle with me for the affair of the afternoon. He said I was too good to use as bait—as Mahomet Khan had intended using me. He produced a pair of my riding-breeches, my helmet, a shirt, and a pair of my riding-boots, that he had stolen from the rest-house at the same time that he'd stolen me; but instead of giving them to me to wear, he made a small boy put them on. His idea was to dress up that boy and send him as bait towards the eastern pass; and although to do him justice Mahomet Khan objected, the fakir had his way. He dressed the boy up, put him across his own saddle, brought out a mob of men carrying dummy loads, and went off towards the eastern pass.

"Their instructions were to show themselves in the bazaar and in every village they passed. They were to talk unwisely, and by this means and that convey the impression that the boy was me, and that the men were carrying machine-guns. And, as a matter of fact, when they moved off, I realised how easily the villagers would be hoodwinked into believing that that boy was me—especially in the moonlight, and when I was supposed to be lying face downwards, unconscious. And when they fired the barracks to bring you down from the pass in case daddy shouldn't ride out to fetch you—well, frankly" —she paused for a moment and shuddered—"frankly, I never expected to see any of you again. I couldn't for one moment imagine how anyone would ever see through a trap so well disguised."

Blake glanced at the fat fakir and scowled. The

mistake he had made lay in underrating the fellow's viciousness.

"He turned back, I suppose, when he had passed through the last village?" he said.

"Yes. Actually, Mahomet Khan would have ridden off with the party in the first instance, but he was afraid the villagers would not recognise him in the darkness. The fat fakir, of course, was impossible to miss—and, moreover, he knew that Jimmy had it in for him over the catafalque business. 'That clever one will follow me to the gates of hell if he thinks I've got his woman,' he said. But Mahomet Khan shook his head. 'We've got the owl to reckon with,' he said, 'as well as the police.' And it was then that he decided to continue the trail right to the eastern pass. I gathered that you were the owl, Mr. Blake?"

"In more ways than one," Blake admitted.

But the information pleased him. It was the last link in his chain. Mahomet Khan had been smart in coining the sobriquet, but in the end it was going to hang him—if only Blake could stop him before he reached the eastern pass.

He reckoned up the start he had got, and his heart fell. Four hours on a sixty-mile journey—it was too much!

It was Tinker who suggested the solution. A kite-hawk wheeling lazily in the sky was really responsible for the idea.

"What about a 'plane?" he asked suddenly.

Blake snapped into action. Of course, a fast 'plane!

"Can we get a 'plane from anywhere?" he asked Miss Kershaw.

"There are plenty of R.A.F. machines in Peshawar."

"Question is: can we get through to them?"

He turned to find Winfield, but the D.S.P. was already racing towards them down the road. His eyes were glazed with amazement. He was gasping like a fish out of water. Looking at him, Blake knew that he had discovered the secret of the ten bales.

"One minute!" he said, when the man would have burst into chaotic explanations. "Never mind about the bales. I want to get through to Peshawar without a second's delay. Can it be done?"

Winfield struggled to get his mouth closed. Stopped in mid-career, breathless with excitement from the discovery of the century, his condition was pitiable, but Blake had his way.

"By helio—yes," he managed to answer.

"Can a 'plane land here?"

"The last one managed to land on the road," Judy butted in.

"Fine!" Blake was jubilant. "Get through right away to Peshawar, Winfield, and ask for the fastest 'plane they've got which can land on the road. Tell them to bring two parachutes." His eyes brightened. "If we're too late this side of the pass, Tinker, we'll drop down on the other, even if it's in his very own village!"

Winfield, literally sweating now from the effort of suppressing his discovery, at once called for his signaller.

"Helio D picket!" he directed. "SOS 'priority' straight through to R.A.F. headquarters in Peshawar." He wrote out the message as he spoke. "There are only three relay posts between here and Peshawar. If they get a move on at the other end, a machine will be here in less than half an hour."

He spoke quickly, breathlessly. He was dying to get back to those loads.

"What do you think they've got there, Blake?" he ripped out when the helio began to flash its message. "By heavens, man, it's the haul of the century. What do you think those devils were taking over there? What do you think they're up to? No wonder we couldn't think what was afoot! No wonder none of us could solve the riddle of the bales! If you thought for a thousand years you'd never hit it!"

Blake smiled at the other's enthusiasm.

"Bolts?" he suggested quietly.

Winfield's peroration was chopped off short. His jaw fell. For a full minute he remained staring at Blake.

"Eh?" he stammered at last.

"Bolts," said Blake again. "Machine-gun bolts. Am I right?"

.   .   .   .   .

Captain James Winfield sat down on the boulder behind him. He tried to speak, but words would not come.

"How long have you known?" he asked at last, his voice flat.

"I didn't know—exactly," Blake admitted gracefully. "It was a guess. I couldn't see what else it could be, seeing that the guns themselves are already over the border. I felt sure that the contents of those ten bales was in some way complimentary to the machine-guns in that old arms dump, and bolts seemed the most likely solution. They are of Russian manufacture, I take it?"

Winfield got up abruptly. This was past everything!

"You don't happen to know the numbers on them, by any chance?" he asked sarcastically.

Blake shook his head.

"No," he laughed. "But you see, Winfield, I happen to know the man who supplied the original consignment to Mahomet Khan—the one you thought was hanged!—and he is a Russian. Or, rather, was a Russian!" he corrected himself grimly.

Winfield stared in amaze. He was to be enlightened later.

"How many bolts are there?" Blake asked.

"Exactly one hundred!" Winfield said mechanically.

Blake gave a whistle of surprise.

One hundred machine-guns! It was almost incredible. One hundred machine-guns might not mean much in a western country, but in a land of muzzle-loaders and obsolete .303's, one hundred machine-guns would spell absolute supremacy for whoever controlled them.

"What are you going to do with them?" Blake asked.

"That's what I'm wondering," he confessed. "They've burnt my barracks, now. I haven't even a guardroom."

"Couldn't you put them in this 'plane, when it lands?" Tinker suggested. "Let them to go Peshawar."

"The very thing!" the D.S.P. cried. "They can be stored in the arsenal there, or completely destroyed—whichever the authorities think best. Yes?" he broke off, as the signaller came running up and saluted.

"A 'plane has started, huzoor. It will be here in twenty-five minutes."

"Good!" Winfield turned to his havildar. "Get these bolts tied up in bundles, havildar," he ordered, "and have the men carry them down to the road on the plain. A hawar-jehaj is coming presently to take them away."

Then the three Englishmen walked back to where Judy was awaiting them.

"By the way," Blake asked suddenly, "you can't get into touch with that eastern pass, I suppose?"

Winfield shook his head. The eastern pass was not in his territory, and the configuration of the ground made helio'ing impossible.

"Still," he added, "they'll probably stop him there, all the same!"

"Why?"

"Well, somebody might recognise him, for one thing! And for another, he hasn't a pass."

Blake smiled. The D.S.P. even now had no great opinion of the arch-plotter's mentality.

"You forget that he has the safe-conduct for the original party," he said. "And even if he hadn't, he'd still get through. If the worst came to the worst, he'd show them his Gold Eagle of the Intelligence Service."

"He'd show them——" Winfield's voice tailed off into bewilderment, then: "Do you mean to say that he's another of those merchants?" he asked contemptuously.

"Masquerading as one, anyway," Blake smiled.

"You mean——"

Tinker gave a funny little gasp. His jaw fell ludicrously.

His eyes snapped wide. For a full minute he stood literally transfixed with amazement.

"Great sufferin' cats!" he jerked out then. "You don't mean—you can't mean—Ali Singh?"

"The canary," nodded Sexton Blake. "It was he who——"

A frightful oath cut sizzling across his explanation. Spinning round, they saw that the fakir was straining in the grasp of three hefty constables. He tried to spit in Blake's face, but the men forced him back.

"Dog—and son of a dog!" he ripped out venomously. "I said at the time that you'd be safer with your throat slit. May Allah blast the flesh from your bones and the sight from your eyes!"

"Oh!" retorted Blake pleasantly. "So you've come to life again, have you?"

But it was only for a moment. For even as the fakir tried to spit again, he was choked by a sudden rush of blood from his throat. He sagged sideways, his mouth twisted into a ghastly grin.

"Dogs!" he gasped out, as his life ebbed away from him. "You'll never—hang—me! Dogs! Sons of dogs!"

"Here's the 'plane!" cried Judy Kershaw. "She's coming down, Mr. Blake."

Blake looked into the sky. A medium-sized, single-engined fighter was sweeping towards them, full out. Her pilot was evidently losing no time.

"What's the panic?" the pilot cried, as he landed.

Blake asked for the parachutes, and motioned Winfield to do the talking. Nothing loth, the D.S.P. gave a hasty but graphic account of the night's proceedings while Blake and Tinker slipped on their harness. Then he turned to Blake. "Where do you want me to drop you, Mr. Blake?"

"I'll tell you when I've seen my man."

"Right! Hop in! You'll find paper and pencil in the pocket beside you if you want to communicate with me at any time. O.K.?"

"O.K.!" Blake called from his seat. "Let her go!"

CHAPTER 21

BLAKE'S AND TINKER'S MIGHTY DIVE

THE air-speed indicator registered 220 miles an hour. The roar of the engine was deafening.

The 'plane roared on. Soon a break in the brown mountains ahead indicated the position of the eastern pass, yet still he could see nothing moving on the road below.

Then the pilot held up his hand, and, having attracted Blake's attention, pointed forwards and downwards. Blake leaned over the side, and sure enough, at an angle of forty-five, a huddle of black specks was crawling laboriously down the thin, white thread of the road.

Reaching for his pad and pencil, he scribbled a hasty note and passed it over to the pilot.

"We'll drop out half-way between them and the pass," it read.

The pilot nodded, and a moment later passed a note back.

"I'll hang around for you," it said. "Maybe I'll be able to land somewhere. I'll drop a message on the guard at the pass to tell them to watch out for you. Good luck!"

Blake nodded and crawled out on to the wing. He gave one look below him, waved his hand, and dived headfirst into space. He went down like a stone, turning over and over sickeningly.

Then Tinker climbed out.

"Cheer-o!" he bawled to the pilot. Then he, too, dived off into space.

The pilot swept round in a wide circle, and his eyes took on an anxious look when those two tiny specks continued their mad career earthwards without attempting to open their parachutes. Then a tiny white cloud blew out above one speck, followed by a second cloud above the other.

Blake landed easily, but went head over heels with the momentum. By the time he regained his feet and looked about him, Tinker was busily disengaging himself from the tangle of his own gear.

"We'd better hide these somewhere, hadn't we, guv'-nor?" he asked, when presently he came up carrying his parachute. "They'll show a long way on this brown sand."

Blake nodded. As far as the eye could see, nothing was moving in all that vast immensity of barrenness. They tucked their parachutes behind a couple of big boulders, and then sat down to work out a plan of campaign.

"Better trip them, I think," Blake decided. "We'll use one of the parachute ropes stretched across the road. If we can upset the leaders, the remainder will be thrown into confusion, then we can hold them up. They're all mounted now, by the way."

"I saw that."

Tinker ran off to cut a suitable piece of rope while Blake scouted ahead up the road. Being so near the mountainous border, the plain was literally strewn with all manner and sizes of rocks. Some appeared to be outcrops from the earth formation, but others had obviously been carried down by glacial action in prehistoric days. Presently he found two that would serve his purpose admirably—one upon each side of the road. And around and between those two rocks they fastened their rope in such fashion that it crossed the road slackly from one side to the other.

"We'll leave it on the ground until the first man is right on top of it," Blake said. "Then we'll lift it a foot or so, when it is too late for him to stop, and let the rocks take the strain."

The road was still empty. Looking down from that 'plane Blake had not quite realised the actual immensity of the distance he was overlooking. Those men might still be miles away.

"How did you tumble to the truth that Ali Singh was Mahomet Khan?" Tinker asked, after a long silence.

"Mainly, I'm afraid, for the simple reason that no other explanation filled the bill."

"But he was helping us all the time! He actually saved our lives—and Winfield's life, too, when you were attacked by Bir Beg's men in the bazaar. He was on our side, guv'nor!"

Blake smiled.

"He was on our side just as long as it paid him to be," he said. "As a matter of fact, looked at in one way, it could be said that Ali Singh had engaged our professional services on his own behalf!"

"What for? How do you mean?"

Suddenly Blake put a finger to his lips and froze. Far away in the distance he had caught the sound of thudding hoofs.

Nearer and nearer came the flying hoofs. It was amazing to Blake that any horse could gallop on such ground. One minute it was deep sand, and the next hard rock. Those country ponies must be mighty sure-footed, he thought.

Fifty yards! Thirty! Ten! He held his breath. Five! "Now!" he called sharply.

The rope came up in the precise second that the first two horses raced past the ambush. There was a sudden tug, a wild lurch, a flurry of hoofs, and the first two horses were down. The rest crowded over them, some falling, some staggering sideways, until that narrow bit of road was an indescribable tangle of cursing men and kicking, plunging horses.

Then Blake stepped out.

"Hands up! All of you!" he roared.

The horses continued to kick, but the struggling men fell to dead silence. Eagerly Blake's eye swept the tangle, and suddenly his heart leapt.

There in the centre of it all was Ali Singh! Ali Singh—with the marks of Bir Beg's knife still on his throat, and his thickened lips telling mutely of the same man's fists.

"Line up beside the road there!" Blake warned sharply.

One man's hand fell to his belt. Blake dropped him on the instant. In the same second, Tinker dropped another for the same reason.

"Come out, Ali Singh!" Blake shouted.

Ali Singh turned, then, and the eyes of the two men met. Blake's were hard as pebbles but cool. Those of the native hot as wind-blown coals.

"So it's you, Blake, is it?" he asked.

"It is I," Blake answered. "You've shot your bolt, Mahomet Khan—in more ways than one. The game's up. We've got your machine-gun bolts in Abbabi Pass, and the fat fakir is dead. You are my prisoner."

"Is that so?" The arch-plotter was speaking in English —speaking softly, in his normal voice, in what the night-watchman's son had called his "Oxford accent". Suddenly he ducked, spat out a sharp order to his men, and as though actuated by a single spring, the entire mob surged forward.

Blake met them with a hail of shot. His guns spat fire in a continuous stream—but he was forced to retreat. Tinker leapt in viciously, emptied both his guns and then clubbed them.

Again Mahomet Khan shouted, and again the remnants of his men leapt towards Blake.

"Watch him, Tinker!" Blake shouted fiercely. For Mahomet Khan had dragged a horse to its feet and was struggling into its saddle. His eyes were ablaze with triumph.

Blake seized a horse and swung himself into the saddle, but the horse tripped over one of its companions and pitched him heavily on to the sand. In a second he was up again, but by now Mahomet Khan was one hundred yards away with Tinker in hot pursuit. Blake looked for another horse—dodged to escape a wild swipe from someone's knife—slipped in a pool of blood and pitched backwards. With a yell of triumph the man leapt in to finish him, but in that self-same second there was a vicious burst of machine-gun fire from the sky, and with a roar like a thousand devils the 'plane raced down to the attack.

Surprised, Blake's assailant looked up. He saw the 'plane and terror shot into his eyes. The next second Blake had lashed out with his free foot and sent the man retching and coughing to his back.

Now the gang was flying. That machine-gun had been too much for them.

Now the 'plane was firing again. Doubtless the pilot had spotted Tinker, and gone to his help. Blake set off in the direction of the sound. A minute or two later he perccived a horseman galloping furiously towards him, and screwing up his eyes against the sun, he recognised Tinker.

The young detective reined back alongside him.

"We've got him, guv'nor!" he said, as he slipped from his saddle. "The 'plane machine-gunned him as he rode and killed his horse. Ali Singh—or Mahomet Khan or whatever he calls himself—shot wallop over its head. I'm afraid he's done for."

"Lend me your horse, Tinker!" he rapped out. "Give me a leg up, will you? Are you all right?"

"Bit scratched here and there, guv'nor—otherwise quite O.K." Tinker answered, as he assisted his chief into the saddle. "I'll run along by your stirrup," he said, as they set off.

It was not far. Presently Blake saw that the 'plane had landed, and a little later he observed the pilot leaning over a motionless figure on the ground.

The pilot looked up as he saw them approaching.

"I didn't get you, did I?" he asked quickly, as Blake slid from his saddle with a grimace of pain.

The detective shook his head.

"No," he said. "You saved me, as a matter of fact. Thanks very much for your timely intervention—things were getting a bit too hot when you decided to take a hand in the game. How is he?"

"Not too good, I'm afraid."

Blake sat down beside the injured man. He looked ghastly.

"Could we get him to hospital, do you think?" the pilot asked suddenly. "I can be in Peshawar in about forty-five minutes, if you think it would be any good?"

"I don't think it would be." Blake could see that the man was mortally hurt. He sat for a few minutes contemplating the face below him—marvelling at its serenity, its fineness, its implacable strength. A curious mixture—this Mahomet Khan! Now that the beard was gone, Blake saw many things that he had not noticed before.

Suddenly the tired eyes opened, and rested for a moment on the lean, clean-cut features above him. He smiled.

"So you—you win?" he whispered. "You win, Sexton Blake?"

Blake was amazed that the fellow could speak at all, much less think. He leaned nearer.

"Can you hear me, Mahomet Khan?" he asked.

The arch-plotter nodded, and smiled again.

"As old hymn says——" He was beginning sardonically, but Blake cut him short.

"You killed Gerald Newman, the shipping clerk, in Water Lane, London—didn't you?" he asked sternly.

For a time there was no answer. For several minutes the man lay with closed eyes, breathing stertorously. The pilot ran over to his machine and came back with a flask of brandy, and after Blake had forced a little between his stiffening lips, Mahomet Khan revived a little.

"You killed Gerald Newman, the shipping clerk, didn't you?" Blake asked again.

"Yes." He was smiling again now. "Also Bir Beg—he insulted my izzat! Likewise that faithless dog of a Russian, Paul Verislov. Oh, many men have I sent screaming down to hell, Sexton Blake—and all to the same end."

"Those guns?"

He shook his head.

"Power!" he breathed. "Power!" he repeated a moment later. "The thing I have sought all my life.

Power! The power to lift up—the power to cast down. 'Yea,' I would say, and a man might live. 'Nay,' I would say—and he should die. Power!'' He rolled the word over his dying tongue, as though even now tasting its savour. His eyes gleamed hot as though even yet that power lay within his reach. His whole frame tautened until he was like a drawn sword, shaking himself in the face of Destiny. "Power!" he whispered ecstatically.

Blake moistened his lips again with brandy.

"Who was hanged instead of you?" he asked, when presently the man opened his eyes again.

For a second Mahomet Khan looked at him, and his mouth quivered.

"So you know that, too?" he whispered. "I was afraid of you from the start, Sexton Blake. I was afraid of you all along, but I would not have you killed, not even when I had the chance. You saved me from that faithless one, Bir Beg—and Mahomet Khan pays his debts, Blake. Always he pays his debts."

"Yet you did not pay for those guns!"

"Because that dog of a Russian cheated me," he whispered passionately. "He brought out those guns without their bolts—as though he were dealing with a jungli— an ignorant country lout." He tried to spit, but the effort was too much for him. "Verislov planned to cheat me," he went on presently, "but we planned to go one better. We planned to steal those guns from their hiding-place, and then provide our own bolts. We planned to secure every one of those hundred machine-guns without disbursing one single anna of our capital. I was to go to Russia, buy more bolts, and bring them back here—but in the meantime my brother allowed himself to get caught."

Blake's mouth tightened. Now he saw what had happened.

"It was your brother they hanged, then—not you?" he asked swiftly.

Mahomet Khan nodded.

"My brother," he said. "He had to die, anyway, but knowing that I held the secret of those guns and knowing that I alone was capable of going to Russia to buy more bolts—for the izzat of our house he proclaimed himself to be Mahomet Khan, and so killed two birds with one stone. They hanged him as Mahomet Khan, and soon the hue and cry died down, leaving me free to continue my work. They were only too pleased to hang him. They did not know me. What is one Saiyid chief more than another? But his name shall not be forgotten among my people! He died a shameful death—but he died for an ideal. He died for the izzat of his house—for Islam!—for power! And although those guns will never speak now, Blake—although the banner of our house will never lead the Star and Crescent to victory—none will ever find them. They shall lie where they do lie—safe from pilfering hands! Allah alone knows what they cost! Allah alone shall guard them."

His voice dropped to a mere whisper, to a thin thread of sound that scarcely fluttered his lips.

Blake saw that he was sinking. Bending over him, he put his last question.

"Where is the real Ali Singh?" he asked. He put the question again, and yet a third time, before the sense of it sank into the dying man's brain.

It was then that Mahomet Khan smiled for the last time.

"Down a Poona well!" he almost chortled, and fell back against Blake's shoulder.

The others thought he had gone, but Blake shook his head. Mahomet Khan—murderer, gun-runner, thief that he was—was yet a Saiyid chief and a Prince of the Blood, and he would not die without professing his faith.

It came a moment later. Suddenly, with a last supreme effort, the man raised his face to the sky. "In the name of Allah!" he cried loudly. "There is no God but Allah, and Mahomet is his true Prophet!"

Then his head fell back, and with a long shudder the soul of Mahomet Khan fled to his Maker.

CHAPTER 22

CONCLUSION

THAT evening, after dinner in the rest-house, Winfield, Judy Kershaw, the doctor, and Tinker, sat listening to Sexton Blake.

"The story you already know," he said slowly. "It all began when Mahomet Khan ordered one hundred machine-guns from Paul Verislov. The Russian delivered those guns, but retained the bolts as security against payment; and in the interim, Mahomet Khan's brother was caught in dacoitry and hanged under the name of Mahomet Khan. Whether or not Verislov knew of the deception, I am not sure. I don't think he did, at the time, because as soon as he could—after hearing of the event—he got into touch with Bir Beg and offered him the whole consignment. Bir Beg agreed to buy the guns if Verislov would give him delivery in Famipur, and between them they excavated that tunnel and made everything ready for their reception there.

"Meanwhile, Mahomet Khan had raided the secret dump at Peshawar and stolen the guns. By some means or other he managed safely to run the whole consignment across the border—and now needed only the bolts to make everything complete. He decided to go to Russia himself and buy those bolts—and he did, as we know. But in the interim, Verislov's suppliers in Russia smelt a rat, and notified Verislov of Mahomet Khan's activities. By that time, Verislov had discovered Mahomet Khan's treachery, and he saw at once that his only chance of ever getting a penny for those guns lay in stopping Mahomet Khan and the bolts when the latter got them to India.

"Well, as you know, they did that. Advised by their spies in Bombay that Mahomet Khan had landed with the stuff, they wrecked the train outside Battock Station and secured the bolts from those ten bales. The position was now one of complete stalemate. Verislov and Bir Beg had the bolts, but Mahomet Khan had the guns. It was inevitable, of course, that they should clash. They did clash. But try how he would, Mahomet Khan could not find out where those bolts were hidden."

"So he joined us!" Tinker interjected with a grin.

"So he joined us," Blake agreed. "He could not find the bolts himself, but he thought we might, so he decided to come along with us."

"He took an appalling risk!" Winfield muttered.

"Actually, he didn't!" Blake corrected. "Though even if he had, the position justified it. When Tinker and I arrived in Bombay, Mahomet Khan was at the end of his tether. Through his spies in the telephone exchange he knew that we had come out to arrest him for the murder of young Newman. He knew that our search for him would inevitably land us in Famipur, and he knew that we should finally discover that it was Verislov and Bir Beg who had wrecked that train. Perhaps he flattered us —I don't know. But, in any event, he credited us with the ability to succeed where he had failed. He felt that we should find those bolts—and he wanted to be there when we did find them!"

"But the risks, Blake!" Winfield insisted.

"There were no risks. The proof of any pudding lies in the eating, and the fact remains that no one ever did suspect him. You see, to begin with, none of us knew him. All we knew about the Secret Agent Ali Singh was what Christie had told us—and the man who joined us at Agra was, in every respect, just that man. He was Ali Singh. He spoke as we had been warned Ali Singh would speak. He acted as we had been warned he would act. But the best turn of all was that beard of his.

"That was a masterpiece! He had to come here disguised, because both Verislov and Bir Beg knew him. At the same time, he did not dare to risk my discovering that his beard was false. He told me so, and straightaway disarmed all suspicion. I thought that he was disguised in order to prevent people here recognising him as Secret Agent Ali Singh. Instead of which, of course, he was disguised to prevent them from recognising him as Mahomet Khan. That beard of his was an absolute stroke of genius. It deceived everybody. And the absolute efficacy of the disguise lay in the fact that everyone knew it was a disguise. And knowing that, none of us gave thought to the real identity of the person it covered."

"But he helped you so much, Mr. Blake!" Judy protested. "He saved you from those snakes in the Bombay Mail, and he saved you and Jimmy again when you were attacked in the bazaar——"

"Of course he did!" Blake smiled. "He had to, don't you see? We were no good to him dead. He wanted us to find those bolts for him. He had to protect us!"

"But he told us so much, guv'nor! He nearly gave himself away in unfolding his knowledge of events," Tinker put in.

"For exactly the same reason," Blake answered. "His object was to let me know all that he knew himself—but he had to do it piecemeal and progressively in case I should smell a rat. His immediate job was to put me in possession of all material detail that would enable me to solve his problem. 'That's the data of the case', he said in effect. 'What do you make of it all?' And there again, of course, he was helped by Ali Singh's reputation—the real Ali Singh, I mean. Christie had told me that Ali Singh was a remarkably astute man—and when he showed himself to be a remarkably astute man, well, I accepted it. And eventually I led him to what he wanted."

"To that well, you mean?"

"To the well," Blake nodded. "Actually, of course, he followed Tinker and me that night to keep an eye on us. He guessed from those photographs he saw that I had got a line on Paul Verislov, and that made him nervous. He was not sure how much I knew. It was he, in fact, who fired that pistol into the shop—if it had been Bir Beg's man he would have shot at us, not the candle. But all Mahomet Khan wanted to do was to break up the conference before Verislov had time to tell me that the first Mahomet Khan and the second Mahomet Khan were actually one and the same man."

"How did Mahomet Khan come to know that Ali Singh was going to join you in Agra?" the doctor asked.

"Through his spies in the telephone exchange, doctor. Curiously enough, I warned them down there that their wires were being tapped—but it never struck me that the wire to Poona would be tapped and that Mahomet Khan would be put into possession of all Christie's instructions to the Intelligence there, and to Ali Singh himself. I remembered it later—when I had come definitely to suspect the man—but at the time it quite escaped me."

"But why should he tap the Bombay wires?"

"To keep himself au fait with the latest police developments, doctor. You see, prior to my own arrival in the country, Mahomet Khan was hoping that the secret police would solve his problem for him, but they didn't. They were as bewildered as he. That's why he was hanging about in Bombay while his lieutenant, the fat fakir, was holding the fort at this end. And that's where he did for himself. As soon as I learned that the fat fakir was Mahomet Khan's agent, and that it was the fat fakir who had received that wire about the 'owl'—then I knew who he was. Yet he had to make it clear that the fat fakir was Mahomet Khan's lieutenant in order to make absolutely sure that you looked into that catafalque, Winfield. He was between the devil and the deep blue sea, just then."

"How do you mean?"

"Well, as soon as he heard of the projected funeral party—and he knew of it long before we did—he saw in a moment how Bir Beg was going to take those bolts out of the country. His first notion was to attack the catafalque after it had gone through the pass, and to that end he had his men, under the fat fakir, waiting across the other side. But then he reasoned that if he could tumble to that

solution, I could, too. And he saw that I might stop the
catafalque this side of the pass and rob him finally and
completely of every bolt he had brought out in those
bales.

"That scared him. Rather than risk that, he would not
allow the bolts to be put into the catafalque at all—but
how could he prevent it? So far, you must remember, he
still had not discovered where the bolts were hidden; but
he had a shrewd suspicion that wherever that dead holy
man was lying, there, too, would be the hundred machine-
gun bolts. In that event he would have to wait until the
catafalque actually arrived at its destination in the bazaar
before staging a fight for possession between his own men
and those of Bir Beg."

"A risky proceeding, that!" smiled the D.S.P.

"Too risky," Blake agreed. "So he planned another
scheme. He aimed to eliminate both Bir Beg and Verislov
at the last moment, seize the bolts, put the holy man into
the catafalque, and send back the funeral party to the
border. You and I were to be induced to look into the
catafalque, knocked on the head, and removed bodily
with the holy man across the pass. That, he rightly
estimated, would throw the police into complete and utter
confusion.

They would come down from the pass to search for us,
thus leaving the border unguarded. And in the confusion,
he then planned to walk the bolts over the border without
let or hindrance from anyone. That was his second plan,
and to that end he sent instructions to the fat fakir to
scupper Bir Beg's men on their own side of the border,
secure the catafalque, and bring it down themselves. He
further instructed the fakir to talk 'dark' in front of your
corporal, in the hope that the man would smell a rat
and come rushing down to you with his news. Well, the
corporal did that. And standing behind my chair, listening
to everything that was said that night, Mahomet Khan
was able personally to witness the success of his scheme.
He was sure, then, that whatever I might do, you, at any

rate, were determined to look into that catafalque and so play straight into his hands.

"Well, as you know, that very same night we found the tunnel. We found the hiding-place of the bolts—and, incidentally, Mahomet Khan came within an ace of losing everything. He was captured by Bir Beg, and rescued only at the last minute—in return for which he knocked me on the head and had me thrown, bound and senseless, into the tunnel.

"Now he was set. With Tinker helpless, me helpless, and you booked for an early disappearance, everything was splendid. He had already killed Bir Beg, and Verislov he must have disposed of during the night. But he still would not risk putting the bolts into the catafalque. The fat fakir wanted to have me killed, but Mahomet Khan refused. At the last moment, however, in case I should break my bonds, he had Tinker put into the catafalque so as to give me something to keep me busy should anything unforeseen occur before he was ready to run the bolts.

"But I escaped. And we rescued both you and Tinker before they could get you across the border. That, of course, compelled Mahomet Khan to think again, and in the end he kidnapped Miss Kershaw and used her as bait to bring us down from the pass. The rest you know."

There was a long silence.

"When did you first suspect Ali Singh of being Mahomet Khan?" Judy asked curiously.

Blake thought for a moment.

"I don't know that I ever did suspect him," he answered rather unexpectedly. "But the beginning of the end was when I found Bir Beg dead in his house. The previous night, Mahomet Khan—or Ali Singh as he was then—had gone back to the cellar to fetch his Gold Eagle of the Intelligence Service, which he said that Bir Beg had taken. It was a matter concerning his izzat, he told me a bit stiffly, his honour. Actually he had gone back to kill the man—and I asked myself why. I proved that he had killed the man when Tinker told me that he had not heard

Bir Beg's voice in all the time he was in that house. He had not, of course, because Bir Beg was already lying dead in the cellar, and Ali Singh was in control of the place.

"I saw, too, that Bir Beg had not recognised Ali Singh as a secret agent, but as his own self, Mahomet Khan. And the question he was trying to torture him into answering was not 'Where is Mahomet Khan?' but 'Where have you hidden the guns?'

"But the final link was when you told me that the fat fakir was Mahomet Khan's lieutenant. Then I knew. I knew Ali Singh must be Mahomet Khan, because I knew that it was Ali Singh who had sent that wire to Abdul Aza to be passed on to the fat fakir."

"You mean the one about the owl?" Winfield asked.

"That's right. 'Arriving with owl tomorrow,' it read. And it was signed 'Canary'. It was a message from Mahomet Khan to his lieutenant, the fat fakir, warning him that he had joined up with me. The other one, the one we've never heard about from Bombay, contained a message to the same effect. It read, if you remember, 'Father pleased with new son. Baby doing well,' and it was signed 'Mother'. That was addressed to another of Mahomet Khan's watchers in Bombay, and was meant to assure him that the impersonation had succeeded."

"What made you think that the two Mahomet Khans were in reality one?" Winfield cut across an exclamation from Tinker.

"From otherwise unexplainable incidents," Blake answered. "Mahomet Khan was recognised immediately upon landing from the *Nuralia* by a man who said that he was from the same village. He pronounced his name, and said that he hadn't seen him for a long time. He was, apparently, taken aback, surprised, startled. And the next day he was found strangled. When we tried to question a friend of his as to which village the man meant, he, too, was promptly found strangled. I caught the impression that Mahomet Khan was afraid for his identity, and so it proved."

"One moment," Tinker asked. "How did you know that it was Ali Singh who had sent that wire about the owl?"

Blake's smile broadened.

"He had a queer sense of humour—that one!" he said. "He signed himself 'Canary', and the chief function of a canary is to sing. They always sing, don't they? Think of it for a moment. Ali Singh. Ali sing. Al-lee sing—as a velly ploper Chinaman would say. Got it?"

Winfield roared with laughter. He remembered that when he put in his official report of everything that had happened. He remembered it again when, several months later, he wrote to Sexton Blake informing him of his marriage to Judy Kershaw, and of his impending promotion.

"Though, in spite of what you told them in Bombay," he wrote, "they still don't believe that it was I who solved the problem!"